CRITICAL ACCLAIM FOR *VERGE*

"Children harvest organs, janitors build magical worlds, and mourning lovers drive to destinations unknown in this searing, precise collection." —*Vogue*

"Bracing [and] profound." —*Entertainment Weekly*

"Yuknavitch is one of the most celebrated contemporary writers. [Now she] returns with a collection of short stories that embody her unique blend of the unsettling and the delightful."

—*Electric Literature*

"The powers of her prose [are] on full, incandescent display. . . . The damaged beauty of these misfits keeps the reader leaning in."

—*Time*

"A vertiginous and revelatory book whose characters—sometimes in desperate situations, and sometimes, finally, in a place of safety—have much to say about the world that we live in now. Lidia Yuknavitch is astonishing." —Kelly Link

"At several points while reading *Verge*, I found myself curled into a ball, my fingers gripping the pages so tightly they almost tore the paper. It was as if the words had crawled off the page and under my skin." —Cornelia Channing, *The Paris Review*

"Diverse and impactful, unlike some collections, where only a few stories shine . . . *Verge* boldly asks some pressing yet unspoken questions, such as: How is it that Americans can say anything with a straight face? Does it hurt more to keep the secrets or [to] tell them? It also forces us to acknowledge—and even embrace—the unsettling answers." —*San Francisco Chronicle*

way the book brings us to the verge of the unthinkable, and then leaves us to ponder our complicity, is astonishing." —Jamie Quatro

"Disturbing and delightful all at once." —*BookRiot*

"With the publication of *Verge*, Yuknavitch's writing flies into hyperspace. . . . [*Verge* is] an act of courage and urgency. The book is historically specific, yet ultimately timeless." —*The Brooklyn Rail*

"*Verge* is a wonderful, challenging book. I know these people. I know their dilemmas, and where I don't recognize them, I believe them. The passion Lidia Yuknavitch brings to the page is astounding. I am caught up, shaken up, and now and then simply delighted. 'Listen to this,' I call out to friends, and then, minutes later: 'No, wait, listen to this!'" —Dorothy Allison

"The stories in *Verge* swim with ravishing sentences, and swimming is an apt metaphor because Yuknavitch's long and multifaceted history with swimming shows up all over her writing. It's there in water imagery, it's there in characters who endure, it's there in the literal text that seems like it's moving and breathing." —*Cascadia Magazine*

"Brilliant . . . Consistently incisive, with sharp sentences and a barreling pace . . . This riveting collection invites readers to see women whose points of view are typically ignored."

—*Publishers Weekly* (starred review)

"Insistently visceral . . . These howls from the throats of women, queer characters, the impoverished, and the addicted remind us of the beauty and pain of our shared humanity. Gutsy stories from one of our most fearless writers." —*Kirkus Reviews*

"In *Verge*, characters find their meaning and faith in their own bodies, grounded in physicality and anatomy, pain and desire. These stories are daring, provoking, and incendiary."

—*Booklist* (starred review)

ALSO BY LIDIA YUKNAVITCH

FICTION

The Book of Joan

The Small Backs of Children

Dora: A Headcase

NONFICTION

The Misfit's Manifesto

The Chronology of Water

RIVERHEAD BOOKS NEW YORK

VERGE

stories

LIDIA YUKNAVITCH

RIVERHEAD BOOKS
An imprint of Penguin Random House LLC
penguinrandomhouse.com

Some stories have been previously published,
in slightly different form, in the following journals:
"Street Walker" (as "Bravo America") in *Ms.* magazine; "The Garden of
Earthly Delights" in *Another Chicago Magazine*; "Second Language" in
Guernica; "Cusp" in *Zyzzyva*; "Shooting" in *Fiction International*;
"How to Lose an I" (as "Eye of the Beholder") in *The Iowa Review*.

The Library of Congress has catalogued the
Riverhead hardcover edition as follows:

Names: Yuknavitch, Lidia.
Title: Verge : stories / Lidia Yuknavitch.
Description: New York : Riverhead Books, 2020.
Identifiers: LCCN 2018058037 (print) | LCCN 2019000954 (ebook) |
ISBN 9780525534877 (hardcover) | ISBN 9780525534891 (ebook)
Classification: LCC PS3575.U35 (ebook) |
LCC PS3575.U35 V47 2020 (print) | DDC 813/.54—dc23
LC record available at https://lccn.loc.gov/2018058037

First Riverhead hardcover edition: February 2020
First Riverhead trade paperback edition: February 2021
Riverhead trade paperback ISBN: 9780525534884

Printed in the United States of America
10 9 8 7 6 5 4 3 2 1

BOOK DESIGN BY MEIGHAN CAVANAUGH

This book is for Andy Mingo, love of my life;

thank you for always finding me

in the spaces between things.

CONTENTS

THE PULL

IN THE WATER THE SWIMMER FEELS WEIGHTLESS. The blue of the pool fills her ears and holds her body and shuts out the world. Swimming is her favorite state of being. On land, the swimmer can barely breathe.

She was not yet two, the story goes, when she first gravitated toward water. One afternoon, during a family trip to the Mediterranean Sea, she wandered off the edge of a dock before anyone could notice, dropping like a rock into the ocean. Her sister, five years older, dove in after her, pulling her back to the surface. When she emerged, she was smiling, not drowning. She remembers none of this; it's a vivid story her family tells.

But then her entire childhood is like one long story she

doesn't want to hear. The kind of story that makes your chest grow tight as you listen.

She'd rather swim than anything else. She'd rather swim every day than remember a single moment of her childhood. She doesn't even remember the shapes of the buildings in her neighborhood. Home is a blown-up brick in her throat.

There is one family photo left hanging in the hallway outside her bedroom, taken at a long-forgotten family reunion. Between the unsmiling relatives are spaces where others should be standing: An uncle. A cousin. A brother or an aunt. As if the whole family were disappearing one body at a time.

She doesn't love anything more than water, except maybe her sister's face. Sometimes, at night, she smooths the crease between her sister's brows when she has bad dreams, as she has often since the tanks came. And her sister gently traces the cavities in her ear to help her go to sleep when her eyes stay open too late because she's afraid of mortar shells. Her sister is like a lifeline to her. Two girls, twinning themselves alive.

She never has nightmares. What she has, instead, are water visions. As if the water is speaking to her.

Move your arms as if you are free from gravity. Open your mouth if you like, but do not breathe as you breathe on land; rather remember that breathable blue by closing your eyes. Then open your eyes. You can breathe underwater now. We all can. We all did. Before time. Now let your body sink rather than float. When you reach the bottom of the ocean, let your feet find the sand, let your weight come, stand up. From here, you can walk wherever you like. Starfish and turtles are here with you now. An electric eel swims by you, arched like an S, spotted yellow and blue. Look at your hands. Can you imagine fins? Spread your fingers wide. There was a time before fingers, arms, legs. Before the landlife. There is no alone in the ocean. There is only the lifedeath of water. Thriving.

There's another story her family tells, about how swim coaches spotted her in a hotel pool, churning away all by herself. That's how she got onto a swim team. Before the ground gave and the sky began to rain metal. Anywhere there was water, she found it. A kidney-shaped hotel pool next to the supermarket, the ocean on vacations, a bombed-out apartment complex with a half-full pool, leaves and dirt and dust and who knows, maybe blood, too, but she didn't care. She'd swim anywhere. Swimming made the world go away.

Swim practice makes the swimmer feel alive. Her muscles moving her through water, the rhythm of breathing and not breathing, her heart pumping. The only people she feels close to are other swimmers. They don't need a language to understand one another. Underwater all bodies look related, making the same shapes, creating the same rhythms, moving through waves different from one another and not.

Sometimes she wishes she could swim all day and night instead of going home.

But there comes a day after which everything about the swimming pool, and what went on inside her there, is transformed. School is being canceled more and more often, for weeks at a time, but still she and her friends text one another and talk about regular things. Kids tend not to notice change; they just want to be with their friends, to be normal. But there are warnings. There have always been warnings, but on this day her mother forbids her to leave the house for school or swim practice.

That afternoon, while her shoulders ache from not swimming, a screeching comes in the sky and then a deafening quiet, and then a bomb obliterates most of the roof and one wall of the swimming pool. Two swimmers who were friends of hers are killed, their bodies limp at the surface of the water, then sinking. They never swim another lap toward their own futures.

After death comes into her life and takes the water, all she thinks about is making for the ocean.

In her watervision the ocean underneath things hums through the bones and detritus of ships and sea creatures and the bodies of men and women and children and animals and coral reefs blooming and dying and plastic and oil and volcanic plumes . . .

everything fluid, everything part of everything else. Whole civi-
lizations next to new colonies of fish, new species, deeper and
deeper meanings. Photosynthesis and its absence and yet life and
more life. Underwater the death of things giving way to the life
of things. No walls or roads or fences or states or bombs, only
thermohaline circulation, the submarine streams, the impact of
Earth's Coriolis-making motion. Tides pulled and pushed by the
sun and the moon. The sea speaking to you. Her swells and re-
treats. Her creation and destruction and re-creation in endless
waves.

WHEN SHE AND HER SISTER leave their country, they
already know the perils of the journey. Her parents know.
Everyone everywhere knows. The story of how to leave
came alive before they were born. Nightly conversations
between family and lovers and friends and strangers, telling one another about the cleave of leaving. Her foreground
is cluttered now, with her dead friends and the bombed-
out training pool, all of it between her and her freedom to
swim. She has the same desires as all kids: She wants
to swim. Have friends. Go to school. Not to starve. Not to
die. She grinds her teeth.

So when she and her sister leave, the leaving already has
a story. They will join a wave of other leavers. The journey
will move by land to Turkey, then through the Aegean to

Greece, and from Greece twenty-two days to Germany. It won't matter where people are from, what origin their bodies have. It will only matter that they travel together, like a new organism formed in the leaving of a place, a mash of languages and fears and desires. Like a new species emerging from water to shore.

In the Aegean, at dusk, when their raft like so many others around the world begins to falter, they are all so thirsty that salt and skin flakes are forming on their faces and around their eyes and mouths. The others on board are teens as old as she and her sister and much younger; two are infants; some are older. Among everyone there is a fierce sort of kindness, a violent compassion that might keep them all alive if they keep it afloat. When the raft begins to capsize, for a moment it looks to her like a tilted family photograph, as if the world has gone off-kilter and the people are spilling out of frame into the sea. She studies their faces, family of strangers, then looks back at the water.

The hardest part: Everyone in the raft can see the shore in the distance, but she can see on their faces that none of them is swimmer enough to make it.

In her watervision, the swimmer feels the pull.

There is a pull for some people when they are in big water. A pull no one talks about. The pull comes to people whose lives are too weighted. People whose lives break the story and travel to realms everyone else fears. The pull is cool and warm at the same time; it releases a body back to history; it is something like amniotic fluid, only stronger. Most people who feel the pull let themselves go down a little, sink underwater some. They let their arms and legs go limp, and they close their eyes and hold their breath with a superhuman calm. The kind of calm that comes to those people who believe as children that they can breathe underwater. Those who feel the pull then experience one of two things. Some thrash toward exhaustion, then move toward a kind of motionless surrender, as the water enters what used to be their breathing, as it did before we were born. The pull lives in all of us differently.

Then there are the others, who open their eyes underwater and a rush of agency comes into them, much bigger than breath, and they bicep and kick their way back to the surface and pull air back into their lungs in a great gulp. They fight for life.

She removes her shoes in the raft. Her sister removes her shoes as well. She removes her pants. Her sister follows. She slides from the raft into the water. Her sister slides into the water after her. Two swimmers who learned to swim before they learned to walk.

The swimmer eyes the distance, her head a buoy on the surface of the sea. What would look much too far to a regular person—what looks terrifying, like a choice to drown, to the others on the boat—seems absolutely possible to her. She turns to look at her sister. She can see in her sister's eyes that they can both make it. Treading water, her arms making figure eights and her legs pumping easily, she has no doubt in her body. They can swim to life. She reaches over and smooths her sister's brow.

Then the sisters find the raft ropes and tie them to each other's ankles.

With a phenomenal confidence, they swim for it, towing the others behind them. The beautiful bodies of the swimmer and her sister, and the great watery pull underneath, and the pull of the eyes and hearts of the people hoping against hope in the raft, and the pull of the great wrong world raging around them toward—

This story has no ending.

We put children into the ocean.

THE ORGAN RUNNER

FOR SIX MONTHS, WHEN SHE WAS EIGHT YEARS OLD, Anastasia Radavic's entire left hand was grafted to her ankle, just above her foot.

She'd been run over by a combine harvester in a wheat field, completely severing her hand from her arm. Though she'd worked in the fields with her family since she was five and was thus considered skilled as a laborer, a three-second glance away as the combine harvester passed her row of youths, their hands low to the ground, was time enough for the tragedy to occur. The hand was too badly damaged to reattach immediately, so the doctors attached it to her ankle to let it heal, a risky procedure for even the world's best doctors. In her part of the world, the doctors

were often newcomers, eager to hone their skill at the latest procedures in an area with plentiful patients and little
regulation. Six months later, doctors reattached her hand to
her wrist. It took several operations before the feeling returned, the pink color gradually improving with her blood
flow, and eventually she regained some use in the hand.
But she never forgot how it looked growing from her ankle.
Two parts of her body seamed together in a way they
should never have been. She remembered resting in a hospital bed, staring down at the handfoot, wondering if they
told each other secrets.

At night the other children in the state hospital whimpered a little like animals, crying themselves to sleep, some
of them more or less abandoned. This went on for months
and months as Anastasia healed. She thought of her hand,
lodged at her foot, and it made her think of chimps, the
way they run with the backs of their hands to the ground
and their feet grabbing at things for traction. Her dreams
filled with primates; she imagined herself running with her
hands.

Anastasia knew from school that the Soviets had used
rhesus monkeys in their Bion satellite program in the 1980s
and '90s. She had even memorized their names: Abrek,
Bion, Verny and Gordy, Dryoma and Yerosha, Zhakonya
and Zabiyaka, Krosh and Ivasha, Lapik and Multik. Of

them all, only Multik had died, slipping away while under anesthesia during a biopsy.

Anastasia spent nearly two years recovering at the state hospital, and she told any nurse who would listen about her fascination with the monkeys. One of them snuck her a book by a Western primatologist, Jane Goodall—*My Life with the Chimpanzees*, it was called—along with a small stuffed monkey. She slipped the book under her thin, stained mattress to keep it safe.

After her hand had healed as much as it was going to, she was released from the hospital, hiding the book beneath her waistband in the small of her back as she prepared to leave. The stuffed monkey—she'd named it Goodall—she carried openly; it was a child thing, and no one noticed or cared. She was sent back to a distant aunt who agreed to take her when her family didn't show up. (*What use is a one-handed girl on a farm?* her father had been heard to say. *We have nothing but work here.*) She lived in a house with seventeen other children.

The distant aunt (*Was she?* Anastasia wondered), as it happened, made her living from her body. Most of the children were hers. (*Were they?* the girl wondered.) The aunt took great pride in the fact that she'd lost none of her children, to death or anything else. The children ranged in age from an infant, suckling at the woman's breast, to a fourteen-year-old boy. But the aunt was aging, and that tilted the economy toward new endeavors.

Anastasia never returned to school. Instead, she quickly began learning the lessons of the house. As early as five years old, the aunt started instructing the children on a matter that was very important to their survival, or so they were told. The human body, they learned, has eight organs that can be donated to another body: the lungs, liver, heart, kidneys, pancreas, and small intestine. Tissue can also be donated, including skin, bone, tendons, cartilage, corneas, heart valves, and blood vessels. Some organs, including the liver, could be donated in sections. Sperm, breast milk, egg cells, hair. Everything of a body had worth.

After the middleman took his cut, roughly four percent of the donor price went to the organ runner. Four percent isn't much, but multiplied by seventeen workers it meant everything. Enough to buy a new refrigerator or stove or car, enough to change things forever.

Anastasia made a place for herself in the house quickly by immediately abandoning self-pity (a luxury she'd given up the first time she watched her father backhand her mother nearly across the room) and securing a sleeping spot in the front room, in a nook carved into the stone wall near the fireplace—probably used in other centuries for cooking or keeping food warm or babies or hens or who knows what else. She shoved Goodall into the corner with some straw and made herself a pallet from old blankets and newspapers, not unlike the nests made by chimps she'd read about in the Jane Goodall book. It was a good space for a child and a stuffed monkey: safe from harm, warm, close to the door in case she needed to run.

Most of the other children seemed unfazed by her arrival, absorbing her into the organism of them. Except the oldest boy, Kiril, who decided that she was worth his ire, perhaps because she was new and a lame with her barely functioning hand. Children who move through life in packs are skilled at identifying the weak.

Kiril's favorite game was to snatch and hide Goodall, the stuffed monkey. Over time Anastasia grew expert at finding the object quickly by imagining a question: What would a boy whose boyhood has been taken from him do with a beloved object, having never been beloved himself? His hiding places were obvious, sometimes even a bit sad.

But one day something quite different happened to Goodall. As Anastasia was hunting for him, peering under a woodshed outside the house, Kiril came around the corner holding Goodall's arm in the air above Anastasia's head. She lunged for the stuffed monkey but missed. Kiril laughed, and the laugh made a sound something like a child moving toward manhood. Then Kiril brought out a giant pair of metal scissors—the kind that metalsmiths used—and clipped Goodall at the wrist. As he stood there holding Goodall's hand aloft, Kiril's smile curled like a worm. Anastasia's breath stuck in her throat. She ran to retrieve the handless Goodall from the mud.

Kiril held the severed hand out to Anastasia.

"You can sew it to its foot if you like."

She lunged for the hand a second time.

Kiril put it in his mouth and swallowed it.

In her head, Anastasia repeated the names of the cosmonaut monkeys: Abrek, Bion, Verny and Gordy, Dryoma and Yerosha, Zhakonya and Zabiyaka, Krosh and Ivasha, Lapik and Multik. Then, in her head and heart, she vowed to kill Kiril.

The thought came easily to her. A transaction, no more.

Had she been able to retrieve the monkey's hand, she thought later, she would have sewn it to the monkey's ankle for a while before putting it back where it belonged. Proof that anything could be taken apart and put back together. Instead, she simply sutured closed the monkey's arm at the wrist.

ON HIS FIFTEENTH BIRTHDAY, Kiril was thrown something like a party. Poverty and wealth take different shapes in a home. Children who grow up without the support of family or security can become slippery, uncertain, feral.

And yet, compared to abuse or neglect or relegation to an orphanage, their life might qualify as happy.

When Kiril blew out the candles on his cake, he stood up to give a small speech. Lifting up his shirt and pulling his waistband down just a bit, he told the others of his kidney operation, delicately fingering the stitches (which looked to Anastasia like a reddish, fascinating zipper) stretching from near his belly button up toward the side of his rib cage. Then he pointed to the new icebox his kidney had paid for. The aunt smiled. The other children clapped.

Very small pieces of cake that didn't taste like much were cut—enough to feed all seventeen of them, plus Anastasia and the aunt and some man Anastasia didn't know. Then all the children wanted to see inside the new icebox, where frozen meats and breads and vegetables and cheese were stacked like blocks of colored ice. The icebox would change their lives. To be able to store food was to live differently. Anastasia thought briefly of Kiril's red zipper scar, imagined reaching in and grabbing some other organ from inside him as if she were reaching in for food.

A different child, a boy of eight or so—his name might have been Yegor or maybe Iilya; Anastasia sometimes got them mixed up—then smiled and threw his hands in the air, yelling, "These hands! These hands!" Because he'd been the organ runner. For Kiril's kidney. Anastasia stared at his hands in the air, her own deadened hand hanging down by her side.

The organ runner's story always mesmerized the other children. The doctor (*Was he a doctor?*) had placed the bloody bulb of Kiril's kidney into the organ runner's rubber-gloved hands, and then the organ runner placed Kiril's kidney into a picnic cooler filled with precious ice, and then the child ran and ran between houses through alleys through breaks in fencing around trash in the night to an apartment about twenty-seven minutes away (they'd timed the run again and again) and up the apartment stairs three flights and into a dark room where a woman in her sixties from Florida was lying anesthetized on a table, with another doctor (*Was he a doctor?*) standing by, both of them waiting for the delivery. And why child runners are best is their small size their nimbleness running through alleys and slums and refuse and detritus their not being stopped for questioning their looking like street urchins crawling the nightscape exactly as they should look. And children asking nothing just running away.

There were other stories the children told, gathered on cold nights next to the fire. When one of them asked, another would lift a loose floorboard and pull out an old article from the United States—unfolding it carefully, as if it were something to be treasured—and read aloud.

They memorized individual phrases about a faraway person named Kendrick: "Died in a tragic incident at a local school." "Smothered under a floor mat." "Body unearthed." "His organs removed from his body, the cavities filled with newspaper."

Children's lives all over the world are shaped by such tales, told or lived by adults who transgress every principle of human value. Do not get kidnapped or snatched or abandoned, they learn. Everywhere, eyes might be watching you. Your bodies are worth their weight in gold.

Kiril's ire, and Anastasia's hatred, hit a zenith on the night of Anastasia's first run. She'd done the route with a handler a dozen times, always in twenty-one minutes door-to-door with an eight-minute car ride between. Once, when the driver was late at the pickup point—*twenty-three minutes twenty-five minutes thirty-two minutes*—she stood in an alley trying to look like stones in the wall, shifting her weight from foot to foot, and at forty-four minutes she opened the picnic cooler filled with ice and a kidney and slipped her lame hand into a blue surgical glove from her pocket, jammed it down into the ice, and started massaging the kidney. She didn't know why she did it. She just felt that the kidney needed help. Since she had so little feeling in her hand, Anastasia was able to keep her hand in the ice all the way to their destination, even as the driver looked over the backseat saying, *Your hand, your hand, isn't that cold? Can you feel your hand?* Anastasia just sat there, singing quietly to the small kidney, until they reached the apartment and the driver told the doctor (*Was he a doctor?*) and the husband of the recipient—a Jewish woman from New York City whose name could not be moved any higher on the transplant list due to her age—what the girl had done.

And the husband of the woman from New York sat in a chair and cried, because he knew how important the hands of children could be.

AFTER THAT the story of Anastasia massaging the kidney on its journey took on a kind of magic. People started asking for the girl who had such sacred luck with human organs. Kiril repeated the story of his kidney removal, showing off his scar, but the scar was not as interesting as it once was, and it was forgotten in favor of the story of the girl who lovingly delivered organs to grateful recipients. All over the Ukraine and Russia, people began asking for the girl organ runner as a form of good luck. A bit of hope in the dark.

The aunt and the household prospered.

Kiril left rat shit and dog droppings in Anastasia's hole in the stone wall.

Anastasia dreamed of Kiril's death and dismemberment.

. . .

ONE SECTION of the Jane Goodall book that imprinted on Anastasia's brain involved her time as a secretary in a physiotherapist's clinic. The patients there were all afflicted differently. There were babies with clubfeet, children with polio whose limbs were limp and paralyzed, teens withering away toward death from muscular dystrophy or cerebral palsy. Many of the children could not walk and would have to spend the rest of their lives in wheelchairs, or leg irons, or clumsy crutches. And then there were the children whose diseases didn't have a name yet, who could not seem to control their muscles at all, whose arms and legs were at war with themselves. Those children were often labeled crazy and sent to mental institutions. The doctor who treated the patients shared with Jane a surprising story: Once he had told a rather adult joke to a roomful of child patients at the clinic. As soon as he delivered the punch line, one patient's eyes lit up with joy: the girl with the so-called crazy eyes. She was the only person in the room who'd understood the joke. The doctor took the girl home with him and gave her private lessons. The girl turned out to be quite brilliant, learned to talk, and passed every one of her school exams.

Anastasia believed in the secrets of girls. Maybe all girls carried them.

After that, Jane Goodall went to Africa to study chimp behavior.

Anastasia grew the beginnings of breasts.

Kiril approached sixteen years old, the age when the children were no longer children enough to stay in the house.

The week before Kiril was to leave, he caught Anastasia in an alley on her way home from selling hair. He grabbed her by the neck and held her against the wall like that. With his free hand, he unzipped his pants, grabbed her feeble hand, and said, "Do it. Massage my organ." His mouth looked like a line cut with a knife.

For a while she didn't move. Briefly she wondered if it was possible to rip a cock off a body with one's bare hands. She'd once heard of a father ripping his daughter's ear off. Then he tightened his grip around her neck and lifted her a little off the ground, to show her that he could. Her windpipe constricted. This is a stupid way to die, she thought. Silently, in her head, she repeated the names of the monkeys: Abrek, Bion, Verny and Gordy, Dryoma and Yerosha, Zhakonya and Zabiyaka, Krosh and Ivasha, Lapik and Multik. Then he put her back down on the ground and squeezed her neck until, with her unfeeling hand, she obeyed. Her eyes watered, but she stared at him, refusing to release his gaze. In the end, he was the one to look away.

Then he came. Then he ran. Anastasia spit on the ground next to the semen. She looked at her hand, then wiped it on the wall, carrying a small murderous desire up her arms and into the base of her skull.

By THE TIME Anastasia turned eighteen, she had her own crew of four girl children. The aunt, or whoever she was, had agreed to something like a franchise situation. Anastasia earned enough to rent a small apartment for them to share. They all slept in the main room together. Goodall had a position on the mantel above the fireplace.

At night, in front of the fire, Anastasia would read to the girls from Jane Goodall's book. She read to them about how the orphaned chimps who make it to sanctuaries are lucky. About how some infant chimps are sold to animal dealers, smuggled to different countries in boxes that are too small and purposely mislabeled, often dying along the way. About how some chimps are bought to be used in zoos, or as pets for wealthy people, or are beaten with metal bars as part of their circus training. When Anastasia came to the part about medical research labs, where chimps are forced to live in tiny cages and undergo medical experiments, she'd read very slowly what Jane Goodall wrote about how chimps feel pain and fear and experience depression and most other human emotions. Now and then, as she read, one of the children would look up over the fireplace at Goodall.

Anastasia would end the stories by reminding the girls that the United States of America had retired nearly four hundred medical research chimps, many of them returned to live safely in sanctuaries. The United States, a place they all hoped to reach someday.

One afternoon Anastasia was called on a special mission that required herself and one other girl. The organ donation was a kidney—that was not so unusual—but the donor would also be donating a piece of liver for a different patient, and thus a second organ runner would be needed, to be sent off in another direction. In addition, the donor would need some kind of special care for twenty-four hours—just observation, they promised—but a kind of body sitter for a night and a day. The price was unusually good. The recipient, who was from Miami, Florida, had asked for Anastasia specifically.

When she arrived, Anastasia knew that something was not quite right. She could feel it in her neck and spine. The building had no other inhabitants; the stairwell lights were burned out, and the wooden walls smelled moldy and putrid. A voice at the stop of the stairs said, "Come." Anastasia paused, but she knew the money was enough to get the two of them more than a refrigerator or stove. It might get them out forever. With her strong hand, she took the other girl's arm. With her feeble hand, she fingered a knife strapped to the outside of her leg, underneath her dress.

At the door at the top of the stairs, a woman ushered them into the main room of a dark and rotting apartment and then into a bedroom. In the bedroom were a bed, a dim-bulbed lamp, a man standing there with surgical gloves and a tray of operating items, the organ recipient on the bed prepped and sedated, and a cage of the size one might need for a wild animal.

Inside the cage was Kiril.

Anastasia did not blink. She let go of the girl and said, "Where is the donor?"

"There," said the man who would perform the surgery, pointing to the cage. The woman said something in Ukrainian, some kind of warning.

Anastasia stepped closer to the cage. It did not take long for her to see that Kiril had been beaten. Badly. One of his eyes was swollen shut. He held one arm bent against his body like a broken wing. His mouth was bleeding. When he looked up, she could not tell if he recognized her. He made a sound like an animal in danger or a person whose wits had left him. Not a bellow, not a whimper, but something in between.

What she knew was that Kiril had only one kidney.

What she knew was that removing the other would kill him.

Kiril had been captured, it was clear. In this room, his worth was less than nothing. Whatever money—that thing more valuable than a body, or a people, or a nation—had changed hands was worth more than the life of one homeless creature in this newsless, powerless, invisible country.

She looked at her own hand. The feeble one. The one they expected her to use to preserve a human organ before it was sewn into a foreign body from some other world.

She reached out to Kiril in the cage. He put his face against the metal. She touched his skin with the back of her feeble hand. He whimpered.

Kiril would die, but not by her hand.

Or he would die by all of our hands.

When Jane Goodall saw Louis Leakey discover his first ape skull during an archaeological dig, she thought about how that ape had stood right where they were standing, had felt the air on its skin and the sun and the good dirt—how the ape had inhabited the same world in the same spot, as if time and evolution were nothing. It existed, and then it did not.

Anastasia thought of all the girls in the world who make transactions toward life away from death, buying time, buying hope, buying a chance or a way out. She thought about all the boys with the power to stop them with a hand to the throat, or with a dollar or a whispered word. She thought about Jane Goodall, and Africa, and how some monkeys were released into sanctuaries and others were beaten and tortured and others were shot into space. She thought about the United States, those weird and deformed so-called states stitched together from a brutal and bloody beginning, still straining against their sutures, like a hand sewn too close to a foot. *How do any of us evolve*, she wondered, *from out of all this?*

"I'm ready," she said.

STREET
WALKER

FIRST THING IN THE MORNING, WHEN I TAKE OUT the trash, I see it: syringe on the lawn. Still bloody. It spikes and chills my memory: four long years of youth sliding cold silver glint into waiting blue.

My neighborhood is turning. It's not dramatic, it's no more or less real than TV, than other places I have lived, all those little white-lined streets. We can posture as a nation of shock all we want. It's still a story we know: Somebody wants something more than their own life. Somebody else is terrified by all that they want.

It's not possible, in my neighborhood, to tell who has money enough to live on and who does not, though it's clear that no one is wealthy. Old two- and three-story homes built in the early 1900s, with questionable roofs and over-stuffed leaf gutters. Ours a sort of bohemian-looking hippie haven, both inside and out: overgrown garden, cracked eaves, front porch step rotting away. The rest of our street dotted with flat ramblers, faux-stone façades, additions tacked onto additions like berserk extra appendages. One of the houses has been graced with a concrete lion. So regal! Covered in moss and bird shit.

Nor is it possible to tell who is liberal or who is conservative or nuts or brilliant or a criminal or a good citizen. All the façades need new coats of paint, all the yards need care. Even our fences are leaning toward giving up. The spaces between houses hold their secrets: overflowing trash cans and piles of broken flowerpots, garden hoses all snarled up and molding, our efforts at beautiful landscaping creating their own ridiculous labyrinths between our homes. I've noticed that my neighbor Clark and I both wear sweatpants and sneakers after five and on weekends. Clark may be an alt-righter; he may be just a guy who lives in his mother's basement. In our Nike uniforms, who can tell?

In our hearts we meant to complete all the projects, spiff up our neighborhood, improve our homes and selves. In reality we're too fucking tired from too many jobs or kids or just the idea that nothing turned out the way we dreamed it would. Our sad little dream balloons, once swollen with hot air, deflating slowly like my aging breasts.

On the other hand, money isn't what makes our houses homes.

For example, instead of filling my house with things that cost money, I've filled it with things that comfort me: Plates and bowls filled with rocks and feathers and the small bones of animals. Cups with azure beads. Seashells and talismans and trinkets. And books. More books than you can possibly imagine. Books in every room, shelved, on tables, in stacks on the floor.

Books saved me from my former self.

About the only thing of serious value to me inside my house is a vintage Royal typewriter we lugged all the way back from France, imagining that some famous expat writer might once have plunked out something brilliant on it. And a coffee table and a rug I bought when I got tenure—my first non-garage-sale "furniture."

I teach literature in college now. I write. I've become . . . well, we don't say "bourgeois" very much in America, although these days the students love to say "bougie." I'll just say middle-class.

But we all know there's no such thing as middle-class.

IN MY NEIGHBORHOOD they have developed a yearning for the dreaded neighborhood watch. Guy down the street stops me one night as I'm headed home, lead-armed with groceries—he's never spoken to me in his life; I've never even seen him poke his mole skull out of his white house—and he's bobbing his head around like a scared rodent, his eyes darting out of their sockets, so titillated he's sweating. Have you noticed *the problem*? he says. What problem? *You know.* He looks one way, then the other. Go ahead, I'm thinking, no cars are coming, we're on our own street, we're in front of our own houses. He continues: All the *dope peddling.* The drug deals. And that woman being paraded up and down the street, all day all night every day every night. My God, we need to stand together before it's too late. There is a long pause while we consider this. Whose god? I wonder. I feel myself turn on him. Is my neighbor a white supremacist? A fascist? A bigot? A MAGA voter? Then I'm just me again.

Who could miss it? What moron wouldn't notice? Not because they're doing anything *to* us but because they're doing it too *near* us.

The needle against the flesh threatens us with its obscenity, its mechanism of invading living skin.

I carry my groceries back to my house. Clark, my sweatpants twin, the one across the street who lives with his mother and wears undersize rock concert T-shirts and the exact same baseball cap every day of his life, a guy who inherited his money from an accident on the job, a fact that now works him over into bitter and pale and beer-bellied and pot-eyed, waves to me from the other side of the street. Then he crosses and stands on my lawn and says, They'll never change. It's like I always say, once a junkie, always a junkie.

I feel anger welling up in my belly. For an instant I want to hurl my knowledge at him like obscenities. Instead of saying, *Shut the hell up, you ignorant asshole*, I want to scream, *Keats! Byron! Shelley! Van Gogh! Bacon! Eliot! Faulkner!* For some reason I feel a list of M's rise up in my throat: *Mozart, Mingus, Monk, Munch, Miller, Malcolm even!* I want to move on to Germans, Africans, Latin Americans, Russians, French, Swiss, periods, genres. I want to say, *If we didn't have junkies, we wouldn't have art*, but I don't. I just stare at him until he turns away and walks silently back to his yard, his front door, and gone. Anyway, it isn't true. Addiction doesn't make art. Does it? What the hell am I worked up about? It's just *Clark*.

I turn back toward my own house. Then it hits me: We are alike in our silences.

INSIDE, MY HUSBAND is in his ad hoc studio, painting. Just a half room in our old falling-apart house, much like my writing room, carved out of the small space that would ordinarily be a kid's room. We don't make enough to rent him studio space, so we do what we all do: invent ways to live what we cannot have. I set the groceries down with relief—not because I'm tired but because I know he is responsible for dinner, because never again will I have to be responsible for dinner. This is part of my love for him. You'll never know the relief that a junkie or a woman can feel when the pressure of the giant script of Woman or Wife begins to lift.

And he loves me, too, because I can kiss the jagged scars on his wrist like it bleeds a sweet white sugar. And he can butterfly-kiss the collapsed veins on my left arm under all the long-sleeved shirts I wear to work. We are still learning to live in these houses, these lives. We are loving over our outcast and beaten hearts. For the longest time, neither of us could afford therapy, insurance, or any other route to wellness. Today we probably could afford some kind of medical cure for maybe one of us, but neither of us has that much investment in attending to the hard-core addictions anymore, which is just as well. Easier to just keep drinking wine, downing prescription medications, moving potward down the road of our lives. The easy, low-key addictions of homeowners.

Cherise, the neighbor on the other side of us, waddles out to feed her cats. A great lumbering woman who is all heart, as if her body had puffed out from it. Our dog ate one of her cats—well, killed it anyway. We don't know exactly how many more she has over there. We expect our dog will find out. Cherise understands. She goes inside. She will come out at exactly 6:30 a.m., start the Subaru, and go to work. She will come home at exactly 5:20 p.m., park the car, and go inside. On Friday morning, half an hour before the garbage truck comes, she will put her trash in the can. One time, out of the blue, she asks us if we want some poppies. She says she has some bulbs from somewhere in Asia, then lowers her voice: You know, the *funny* kind. I instantly want to fill a bed in my front yard.

I'M SITTING ON THE COUCH, looking out the window, when I see a flash of woman emerge from a space across the street, the alley between a house going to shit and a house being flipped. Right behind her a flash of man. He is skinny with desperation, and she is skinny with fatigue. Both have the ashen flesh of heroin. I've seen them before; I can't help feeling like I know them, in the dumbest way. They are always swearing, usually loud enough to be heard. She is always following him. Up the street, down, up again. I think of the word "cadaverous." I used to think the closer to death you get, that's where the life is. Now I watch from inside my house through a plate-glass window. I hear my husband pissing in the toilet, an ordinary sound, and all I can think is, Thank you, thank you, thank you.

A minute later I see a second guy come out after them,

buttoning his fly. No subtlety, no attempt to hide, just buttoning his fucking fly and heading down the road. How is it that America can say anything with a straight face? I watch the man and the woman turn one way, walking like sticks out of sight. The second man heads off in the other direction.

Withdrawing the needle, the skin slides closed, leaving only a tiny red hole.

Later I'm inside, the living room window just plain glass against the night. Phyllis, across the street, is at it again. She waters her flowers and yard at about eleven-thirty every night. She's bent and rounded in the back from age, but she still looks feisty. She's got her white hair in a sassy little bun on top of her head. Once I saw her march over to the couple yelling at each other on the corner and tell the guy he was just an arrogant loudmouth. He took a step toward her, and she didn't budge, just stood there, all five-foot-nothing of her, with the eyes of a roach: You ain't never gonna get rid of me, buster. I'm gonna live to be a hundred and ninety years old.

Next time I see them, I'm alone in the house, on the living room couch reading student journals. I tell my community college students to write about what scares them. The things they write about are deportation fears and meth-headed relatives and jail and rehab and being a parent too young. My heart is wadding up like paper when

I hear the shouting. I look up. There they are. Just like punctuation. Her face cadaverous. Something in my chest lurching.

I fly out the door, waving at them.

They stop. What the hell does she want? they think. She's not a man.

How much? I say.

What?

How much for her? How much for an hour?

Let's get the fuck outta here, I hear her say.

Look. I've got a hundred dollars. I want an hour. A hundred bucks is a hundred bucks, isn't it?

He looks down the street. He looks at her. She's got *Gimme a fucking break* on her face. She doesn't make eye contact with me once. He peers back down the street, thinks he sees someone, then doesn't. Finally he turns back to me and waves toward her. She doesn't move.

He yells something at her. She's got *Fuck you* on her face. I'm back in my past, inside habits and mistakes, inside things that made me run into fire, but she doesn't know it. Like a transplanted heart, I live on this street, in this life, always in fear of the body rejecting me.

Come inside, I say across the gap between us.

She climbs our wooden stairs and stands in the doorframe, bony arms in a knot across her chest. She has long stringy hair, permed maybe a year ago. Dark circles cupping worn-out gray eyes. Some sweater from 1992. Bell-bottom jeans. Denim jacket tied around her waist. You don't want to look her in the eye, and you can't help looking her in the eye. She looks back outside over her shoulder. I wonder briefly if she sees two lives, two bodies, like I did, like I maybe still do. She comes in, and I shut the door. I catch a glimpse of the man walking away like an ordinary person.

No names—we both understand this.

Sit down.

I don't want to, she says. What the fuck do you want with me?

Sit down.

She sits down.

This is what I, a woman who teaches English all day, think looking at her, a woman who sucks dicks every night but right now is sitting on my couch. This is what I, an ex-addict reformed by something like love and given something to believe in because of books, think looking at her. This is what I, who could not stand to be alone in a room with just me, think: She looks like Mary. This is what Mary must have looked like after Jesus. No way for the body to bear the miracle, the burden, the unbelievable history of nothing, myth. When I see an image of Christ, I picture a Mary so drawn and gaunt and tired and angry and spent to the point of emaciation that she can barely wear her own face.

The Mary on my couch lights a shaky cigarette. What do I think I'm going to do, teach her?

Then she does something that disperses all my idiotic projections. She puts her cigarette out directly on my coffee table, spits on my throw rug. The Restoration Hardware coffee table I bought when I got tenure. The throw rug supposedly from Tibet, though I have my doubts.

I've got this woman in the house. I have one hour. Sometimes all the hours of our life rip open for an instant, then suture back up as if nothing ever entered.

Something in common: You can't stare down a sex worker or a junkie. Either they look away, making you think you're invisible, or they stare through your skull and out the other side, leaving a hole where your psyche used to be, and you're left some hollowed-out moron afraid of crazy people, afraid of ghosts, afraid of your own relentless shadow.

Finally she says, Look, man, what's this all about? You want something? Crack? Horse? Weed? You want me to do something? She takes another drag and quivers like an angel. No, not like an angel. Like an ordinary woman being eaten alive by her own heart, her own veins, her own cunt.

I say, Look, and I step toward her and put my hand near her neck and shoulder as gently as I can, and she says, I don't fucking lick pussy. I'm not into that shit. But I'll play with your tits if you want. I'll finger you.

I look at her for a long minute, feeling stupider than I've

ever felt. I drop my hand to its ignorance. How does one respond to words like that? Finally I tell her, I just wanted to give you a break for an hour. Rest. Eat. Sleep. Drink. Smoke. Do whatever you want. She looks at me like I'm out of my fucking mind. Her eye glances toward the door. I guess you can leave, too, I tell her, if that's really what you want. It could be that's really what she wants. It could be she's hoping this is a way out or up. She stays.

I leave the room.

FOR EXACTLY ONE HOUR, nothing happens. Nothing. And aren't you just a little disappointed? Weren't we all hoping for something else?

Here is what I do: go to my computer and start to write. I don't think I feel benevolent, but I'm afraid I might. I think of things I want to do for her, all of them filtered through my graduate school mind, and I write them down: play her Schubert, wash her hair, give her a foot rub, cook her a real French dinner with six courses, give her my vintage silk dress, watch European lesbian movies with her, read her stories by Colette, paint her fingernails, dunk her in a bubble bath, give her all the money in my savings account, buy her a plane ticket, take photos of her, hold her.

Then I cross every single thing off the list—*stupid stupid*

stupid—shift my point of view like a writer should, and do a rewrite: play her classic rock, shave half her head and dye the other side blue, break into the neighbors' house and drink all their whiskey and steal their prescription meds, get high and watch "Lemonade" on flat-screen on repeat, then take baseball bats to all the car windows lining my idiotic street, *then run and keep running, tits to the wind*.

There is a schism in us all. It shows up differently in every woman, or it dissolves into layers of skin and fat and homeownership, tidy haircuts and well-applied makeup.

I'm really rolling in there. Alone at my screen.

An hour later I come back, fevered with compassion, pumped up from my writing. I've got a character shooting out of me, a story emerging, perspiration lining my upper lip, and she's standing there plain and unimpressed.

S'that it? she wants to know.

Yeah, I say, that's it, trying to breathe like a normal person. And then she's flinging open the door, she's gone, he's waiting down the street with another guy. They walk off, growing smaller and smaller in the window, as if they're walking back to childhood.

My heart like a fist in my chest. What did I just pay for? Was I trying to give her something, or did I just take something, like a fucking john? I eat four Advil and put on my running gear and sit down on my own couch.

. . .

TWO HOURS LATER my husband returns. By then my sweat is just sticky dumb odor. Do I tell him? Once a junkie, always a junkie. Turns out a sex worker and a recovering addict and a literature teacher each carry around the same question in their bodies: Does it hurt more to keep the secrets or to tell them?

I pour us each a glass of Pinot, and he starts on dinner. I like to watch his shoulders while he chops vegetables and sears meat. I like the way the back of his head looks, his long dark hair fastened in a braid or a ponytail like a woman's. I love the spread of his shoulders, the onion and garlic aromatizing the entire house, the sizzling sound of food being put to hot oil. Most of all I love that it's him, not me, in the kitchen cooking.

The nod, the rush, the flood of sensations overtaking a body, the my-god of it, the want of wanting it forever.

I let each sip of wine linger in my mouth before I swallow.

I close my eyes with the swallowing.

I'm holding. I haven't felt this way in years and years.

I still don't know what I'll say or do.

We're deep into dinner when it finally comes.

I paid the woman from the street today, I begin, watching his chewing slow, his eyes adjust to the sentence. It takes him zero time to figure out what I mean. We've seen them out our front window so many times. Watched them like HBO.

You gave them money?

Yes. I paid for an hour of her time.

Like, *cash*?

Yes.

He considers this. He swallows his food. He puts his fork and knife down. It almost feels like one of us is confessing an affair. I mean, not at all, but *kind of.* Something dark and fast and filled with tension shooting up between us.

I pick up my wineglass and drink. I don't know if my cheeks are flushed, but they feel like they might be. My eyes feel alive.

In the house, I say.

Wait, what? They were *in the house*?

I feel his anger rising like quicksilver.

She was.

What the fuck? What the *FUCK*? What the hell did you think you were doing? The questions hang in the air.

Did I think about what I was doing? All I remember is doing it. But I must have. I had the money ready, for one thing. Had I been thinking about it when I got the cash out of the ATM after a grocery store run? But then the drama of an ordinary couple swoops down on us, and he's all, Jesus fucking Christ, do you realize you could have been killed or robbed or hurt—

But I wasn't, is what comes out, and I watch my own arms and hands refill my wineglass, then his, with complete calm. Like I'm taking my chances.

Well, what the hell happened? Now he's standing.

Nothing. I went upstairs and wrote, I came down an hour later, and she left.

He sits back down, almost as if someone has let the air out of him. You're telling me this hooker was in the house today, *alone*, and nothing happened? His cheeks are definitely flushed.

Well, not nothing. Exactly. Come here. I move toward him, grab his hand, and walk him like a pet over to the coffee table. I point to the cigarette scar, and that's when I see it. She's carved something else into the coffee table: CUNT.

My mouth twitches.

Jesus! he says.

But underneath his voice, I can hear desire rising. Danger does that to people whose lives have become normal. It ignites something you thought wasn't important anymore, now that you have a roof over your head and another mammal in the bed every night and enough to eat and wine and a coffee table.

Fear. Fear comes back into us for a moment.

I'm still holding his hand.

Fear + anger + desire = life.

Safely tucked into your house and home and life and marriage can feel dead.

Go down on me, I say.

He starts to grab my hand and head upstairs.

No, here. Right here.

We are on my side of the living room window. The curtains are open to the night.

I AM in the living room drinking Pinot. My husband is in his pretend studio, painting. She's been gone a week. I am watching TV, trying to recognize something.

Then, through the window, I hear the murmur of low voices just out of range: the neighborhood watch. I turn from the images on the TV to the image of the walkers. They've all purchased some kind of DayGlo vests, matching orange caps, Nikes that glow like lowly beacons with every step. Their flashlights swing back and forth with exaggerated purpose. Women with children are packed into the middle of the group, men on the outside. They do not look afraid. They are perfect in their movements, synchronized, brutal. They will cover maybe five blocks north and south and five east and west. Manifest destiny.

I can feel wine bile rising up my throat. I'm about to go get my husband so we can watch them together, so I can puff up and judge them from inside my house and my life—*Look at these idiot zombies, what they need is more fear in their lives, not less*—and then it happens: As they pass directly in front of our house, one of the women in the pack—my god, is it Cherise?—spits with all her might onto our overgrown lawn.

Anger radiates from my face.

Who am I?

User.

Later that night, before bed, I return to the window. There is no one suspicious on the corner now. There is no one dangerous in the alley. The streets are still and empty, a few quiet souls lingering on their porches, no children on the sidewalks. It is the hour of safe and sound. The streets are clean and cured and uncultured—no, that's not what I meant. Uncluttered, I meant uncluttered.

THE GARDEN OF EARTHLY DELIGHTS

BOSCH CENTERS HIS VISION ON THE FOREHEAD OF the clock and says, *Six, twelve, six*. On at six, off at twelve, on again at six, off again, on again. Salmon and sea bass slide beneath hands, his hands palming and fingering the scales and the touch of slime, his breath in the sea and the guts of thousands of slit-open bellies.

There's a new guy next to him, pimply, bleached-blond hair, fingers like an artist's; *he won't last a month, or else he will, he'll be reborn and vex his family.* His thoughts curl around the young man like water. Bosch already wants to take him home. He can't help it. In the small gray-green of things, the young man sticks out like delight. Bosch can smell his hair. His mind's eye is envisioning the man's head resting on his chest, he's thinking of showing him the ropes, how to take care of his hands, how to sleep awake, how to turn the body to cruise control and let the limbs, hands, move themselves, thoughtless. Something about his face. How young in the eyes. How little membranes stretch over the blue eyes, like the film of a fish eye lensing over in sight.

The new man is smoking in the alley after the shift, his left foot up against the side of the building, the cigarette drooping from his lip. His hands are shoved down into his pockets so hard he looks armless. This is what a young man looks like, Bosch thinks, hunched and smoking in the night, his whole life ahead of him but his body resisting itself. Wanting but not. It's too easy to offer him a drink from an inside pocket filled with warm surrender. Easier yet to take him home after maybe ten minutes of not saying anything, just passing the bottle back and forth, their breath hanging suspended in the white-cold night air there before them. Home to a one-room house packed to wood walls with one small black stove, one square white icebox, one makeshift bed, one toilet behind a curtain, one window, asking night.

"Nice place," know-nothing says.

"Works for me."

"Bet you never expected this, huh?"

"What?" Bosch begins the slow undoing of layers of clothing, his skin hot and cold at the same time.

"*This*." The man's clothes shed themselves, his collarbone and shoulders dipping and curving, his hands hanging down the length of his arms.

Bosch thinks and thinks what "this" means. Is it the man before him, his crotch bulging up like prayer between them, the gap of not knowing each other at all luscious and ripe and making him salivate? Or was "this" his whole life, the long wait waiting again and again until new seasons and tides and moons turned the world over? The younger man's lips puff out. Mama's boy, Bosch thinks, only it's a mouthful of bliss.

The room heats up in nothing flat, stars illuminate their naked. Bosch can't see his own hands, but they find the form, working and reaching and sliding their way along. The man is swimming beneath Bosch, he is licking and teasing, he is moving in the underwater of night. Breathing forgets itself back to its blue past. Their mouths gape and suck.

Their two faces point up toward the surface of the night. Bosch tells him about the last guy his age to come through. People saw him out there in the nothingness making a goddamn snowman with his bare hands, frostbite, but the dumb motherfucker didn't know it, pumped himself so full of acid that his hands were two numb clubs, came to work, worked the row without the massive yellow rubber gloves, until someone finally looked over and said, *Jesus God—look at that, he's got meat for hands*. And they took him away with those red and useless weights of flesh hanging from the ends of his arms, and he lost one of them. Couldn't have been more than twenty-two years old.

"That's the trouble," he found himself saying. "You're all fucked up on dope and shit half the time. A guy could get himself into a lot of shit out here that way. There's no room for error. You have to find the rhythm of the place, being here. It's a whole different existence. Don't come to work fucked up. I'm telling you right now. Guys'll take advantage of you, try to mess you up, because when you're out, their pay goes up. All you young guys come out here, college boys, trying to score the big bucks over the summer so you can quit waiting tables during the year, or buy some shitty-ass car, or more dope, or whatever it is you do. Just . . . all I'm saying is, watch yourself. Pay attention. You'll be all right."

The man runs his finger over Bosch's stomach, light as feathers, flesh whispers. Everything inside him—intestines, muscles—squirms and lifts toward the touch.

HE IS IN THE BED of his childhood, in his mother's house. His father has been gone for two years now. His father a no-good his father a cook at a diner his father a clerk at a 7-Eleven his mother needing to feed her baby. It is night. The front door is rattling and cracking and splitting open with his mother and a man. Laughter brings their bodies into the house; he holds his breath, his heart dull-thudding in his ears. He is sweating under the covers from not moving. Not breathing. They careen off edges, furniture, cacophonous, they nearly crash through the wall of his room; no. They are going to her room, to his parents' room, blue walls, blue bed, perfume, and a mirror.

In the morning the man drives away in a Pinto wagon. Bosch eats cereal, his hair a mess, his hands little fists around spoon and bowl. He stares at the milk, the flakes floating there, bobbing up and down, stares and stares at anything but the tired woman entering the kitchen smelling old and distilled and too sweet. Something—breathing?—gives him away.

"What are you looking at, you little shit? Ain't gonna find any goddamn answers in your Wheaties, that's for sure!" Snorts of laughter. "Hey. Mr. Man of the House. I'm talking to you. When are you going to get a fucking job and start earning your keep? I can't keep stuffing your little fat face with food, you know. You're old enough to take care of yourself. Goddamn little suckerfish, that's what you are, a bottom-feeder. Suck suck suck. You make me sick."

Bosch looks up for a slow second before she leaves the

room with a bottle. He sees her eyes magnified and blurry, sees bubbles escaping from her mouth instead of words; his mind drifts away from her without sound, water filling his ears, his nose, his mouth. Only his heart beats out a rhythm. She dissolves from sight until she disappears in a wave of stained silk.

THE MAN'S NAME IS ARAM, and he is out of sight, down and down the line from Bosch. Now and again Bosch can see a patch of his bleached-blond in the corner of his eye, and he is glad. His own flesh seems warmer than before; he can feel his own pulse, and his hands glide and cup and dive between the fish bodies as never before. His neck does not ache in a knot at the base of his head after three hours, his vertebrae do not feel leaded and distorted when he has an hour left, his feet don't throb and spike with the day coming down on them. It's as if his mind is coming back to him in small increments. He sees an image of Aram gently turning in the night, his torso, the muscles of his back barely visible, the fin of his rib guiding his sleep. The salt smell of the sea mingles with his image of the boy, and the image overtakes the present moment. He breathes in the sight, he lets go the work, his body moves without thought, his mind's eye deep in the tangle of memory, or is it the future, coming to him like a pool of water?

. . .

ARAM PUTS HIS MOUTH over Bosch's cock. He can see the woodstove and its little light just behind the boy's head appearing and then not, like that, in the dark of night. His cock sucks thought from his brain. He closes his eyes, and when he comes, it is into the mouth of the world, young and in the shape of an O. He is lost there. A younger man's mouth takes him out of himself. He places his hands on Aram's head, his hair a bright stunning halo. He is caught there for a moment, dazed and electrified.

IN SEATTLE THERE WERE JOBS, but the boys emerging from Issaquah and Chehalis and Sequim were malformed somehow, their bodies twisted away from offices and college degrees. A high school diploma was simply a ticker tape running across his forehead for anyone to see, saying, *I do not speak your language, you must speak more slowly, what are the directions?* Seattle had a different smell, different air—even their hair and shoulders looked different. Contained and quick smart like the click of heels on pavement. When he'd landed a job at the corner bar as a busboy, his mother had said, "That fucking figures. You're exactly like your father, aren't you, pretty boy? I just hope you can do something for a lady with those hands—that's all he had going for him, I can tell you. You got shorted on the brains, and come to think of it, the brawn, too. Nothing in this life gonna come easy to you. You got big lips like a mama's boy, too. I bet you get your nose busted before you're eighteen." And she laughed with the open mouth of a bass, huge and obscene and devouring.

Nights he'd come home and she wouldn't be there, and then she would, him in his world of a room with earphones closed so tight around his skull that his lips puckered, and she'd bang on the door or even open it, swagger in framed by the disconnected air around them, foreign and malevolent. Then she'd cry, or shout obscenities at him.

Other nights men would come, men with hair greased black, slick as a record album and with teeth missing, or with leathery skin and marbled eyes swimming in their sockets. Once, in the earliest hours of morning, he saw her walking naked to the bathroom. Her breasts dropped down like dangling glass globes. Her shoulders sank, as if her spine had given over years ago, her ass dipped in instead of out, and her belly, rotund and hard as a melon, balled out from her spine like a child's. She'd fallen to the floor just in front of the bathroom that morning, and in the bruised light and half consciousness of the vision he'd watched her wriggle there on the floor before turning her head back, contorted and begging, in the direction of his room, her mouth slit downward in a terrible arc. He closed his door, not listening, not thinking. In his bed his mind made waves. *I am weightless, I am adrift and nothing.*

ARAM DOES NOT QUIT. What's more, in the space of half a year, Bosch has learned more about this one man's beautiful body than about any other body in his life. Sometimes he closes his eyes, and he can feel the younger man in his hands.

Hot coffee between palms; dusk.

"Did you think it would be like this?" Bosch says.

"No. Yes. I mean the work. Yes."

"And this?"

"You?"

"Me." He signals nothing in his eyes, just sits there looking at the beautiful man in his one-room world, this fire-headed boy who gives light to a dark making.

"No. I didn't figure there would be anyone like you out here. And I wasn't thinking about anything . . . well, happening." Aram slides from his chair to the edge of the bed where Bosch is sitting like an old beast of some sort. Hunched over and quizzical in the face. He entwines himself—arms, legs, torso—in between the lines of Bosch's body, the spaces where limbs move away like fins. He makes soft cooing noises.

Bosch closes his eyes and focuses on this feeling, so

he'll remember it when it's gone. For it will be gone, will it not? That is the way of things, that is time, and time is a fucker, and except for this one time in all his life he'd never cared about the boot-sludge drone of time, and suddenly it is everything, isn't it? It is the whole of life and death stuffed into a tiny room with not enough oxygen to breathe or keep a fire going. It is strange to be remembering before the thing itself is gone from you, strange to have that pressure to fold images and impressions into the gray labyrinth of brain. Picture them over and over in the mind's eye, day and night, like the never-ending glow of white on white in winter in Alaska.

"I want to know you. I want to know every inch of you," Bosch says, almost begging.

"But we do know each other," he says, grinning. "We keep knowing each other more and more." And he traces lines on Bosch's back, up and over the shoulder to his chest and heart, as if he knows the way, knows it by memory every vein, every scar, every road of skin or thought since before he was born. Bosch's heart beats too heavy in the chest, it tightens and squeezes into a hard ball. His face twists as if he might cry, then releases itself. He remembers himself as a boy and then grinds the memory gone with his teeth.

What is a boy?

. . .

HE HAS A BLACK EYE, a shiner from a man he's never met except in the hallway of his mother's home. For no reason he could tell, just there at the wrong time, wrong place, sledgehammer-hand big man drunk coming down the hall at him saying, "What the fuck are you grinning at?" Alone in his room with his stinging face pressed against the wood grain of the door, he hears them arguing, the rise and fall of voices, the thud of fists or something breaking, a glass, a rib. She is all mouth, his mother, she can rage on with the best of them, she doesn't flinch, she's gutsy that way. But then he hears her incomprehensibly quiet. Even with his whole head against the door, he hears her not at all. He hears the lumbering dull and swollen-thick man banging his way out of the house, wall to wall to floor and slamming out, Camaro screeching away. Nothing nothing nothing from the other side.

Sweat forms on his upper lip. His face is swollen and wet and white. He bangs his head gently against the door.

"Mother."

Nothing.

He opens the door to his room and crosses the hallway to her room. He opens her door. There she is, as he pictured she would be, curled out on the floor, her mouth bloody, her eyes puffy, her peach satin negligee twisted up her torso, the blue of the shag carpet floating her still body.

"Mother."

He helps her up, walks her to the bed. She is not dead. Just submerged and bleary-eyed, mumbling and slurring. "I've got to get it out of here," she says.

"He's gone now," he tells her. "I'll lock and bolt the door. He's gone." He puts ice in a dish towel and soap on another. He washes her face and holds the cold to her eyes and mouth.

Her lips bulge and the words keep spilling out, she shakes her head no and no. "Out of me, it's in there." He thinks, what is it like for a woman to get fucked like that? It is foreign to him. Nothing about her seems like him.

After she swims toward sleep, he goes back to his room. Just before dawn he thinks of icecaps and the white expanse of Alaska. He thinks of an ocean bearing us all away into an arctic otherworld.

THE YOUNG MAN takes off his hood, unzips his gigantic red parka. The down shape of him shrinks, as if he is removing layers of himself, like a Russian doll within a doll within a doll. He pulls his wool sweater over his head by reaching at it from the back. His hair ruffles. He unbuttons the silver tabs on his Levi's, popping them all in one swift pull from the top. He stretches his torso down and up to take off his T-shirt; his nipples harden instantly. His lip quivers for a moment. He inches his long johns down goose-pimpled legs, over muscle and knee and bone to ankle, twists each foot out. Down go his boxers. He is a naked man at the beginning of his life. He is beautiful and almost absolutely still. His breathing is the only thing that moves. Bosch feels as if he might weep. Bosch smells him: sweet sweat and soap and skin. His cock grows, pulses up red between them. Bosch's mouth is watering, and his hands ache at the ends of his leaded arms.

He wants to hold him like an infant, he wants him to suck at his tit while he rocks him and squeezes his cock. He pictures an almost perfect medieval painting of Madonna and child. He nearly vomits from desire before he reaches out to touch him.

They wrestle-fuck on the floor. As Bosch is driving into him, he is also handling his partner's cock in front. Aram arches his back so hard that his head tucks between Bosch's shoulder and neck; he can see his face, contorted angel. Aram comes first, all over himself and all over Bosch's hand; Bosch can see the milk-white spray, and his own release pulses out of him and up inside. Aram says he can feel it in his spine and lets out a kind of laugh, glorious. He says, "I want to stay like this forever, I never want anything to change, it's this I waited my whole life for, this feeling." Bosch thinks sentences give us hope in all the wrong ways, language tortures us into faith.

What's true is that they can only stay like that on the floor until the heat begins to die in the room. Eventually Bosch has to get dressed, go out to the woodshed, and refill the woodstove. He leaves Aram, thinking, He'll get into bed, and then we can sleep for a few hours. He leaves Aram inside but keeps the smell of him sucked nearly all the way to his heart as he enters the white outdoors.

WHEN HE AWAKENS, Bosch hears birds. He thinks of a boat taking him to Alaska, of seagulls. But then it is not birds. It is fainter, human. Soon he recognizes it as the little whimper of a boy; no. It is his mother whimpering. He goes to her room. She is not there. He goes to the sound. She is in the bathroom. It is barely light. Something smells wrong. He does not want to open the door, and then he does, and there they are on the white floor, mother and child, a little red-and-blue lump of fetus curled near her. Five months, six? His mother is so pale she looks dead. As if she'd run out of oxygen hours ago. Her mouth opens and closes. Her hand twitches for an instant. He bends down and looks at things. It is a boy. It was.

.   .   .

AT THE WOODSHED it is clear that more wood needs splitting. Bosch considers not taking the time, then remembers how much Aram likes to sleep, decides that an hour will have no meaning to a beautiful sleeping man. Let him dream. Let sleep take him below the surface of things. Let the image of death be reborn, every single night. With each heave he lets loose a terrible and mindless sobbing. He fills his arms with wood; there is no weight heavy enough to release him.

With arms full of wood, he has trouble opening the door, but then it gives, and a great whoosh of warm air hits the incoming cold. It's a wonder that lightning doesn't form from their meeting like that, Bosch and Aram, two men at different ends of something, or some electrical charge, some white spark crackling between inside and outside. There he is, unmoved on the floor where Bosch left him, a beautiful pale smile on his face, his eyes closed, lashes painted down onto cheeks. His arms are stretched out on either side, his blue veins making rivers across his infant-thin skin at the wrists. Bosch thinks, There is no other heaven than this, this is heaven on earth, and he closes the door and builds the fire like a new faith for all the white against them.

A WOMAN OBJECT (EXPLODING)

GODDAMN IT TO MOTHERFUCKING HELL, SHE SAYS.

I think that ought to cover it, he says. He asks her why she feels the need to swear so much, so deliberately, what depends on it, why it's so important to her. Why, after so long, she hasn't grown tired. Worn out in the mouth.

She looks straight into his eyes, straight into his skull, says, *Fuck you*.

It's curious, he says, because now when she uses profanity, it sounds like everyone else's ordinary speech. Like when she says, *Goddamn it*, she may as well be saying, *can you let the dog out?* or *I'm going to check the mail*. She wouldn't say she's angry, but her eyes flash hard at him for saying this, as if her language did not disrupt, did not slice open the air and slash him across his goddamn stupid too-beautiful face. She knows he is lying. The simple truth is, he was raised Baptist in some shitty little West Texas town, and she was raised in a fucked-up place called Father. His hands are beautiful. Her mouth is potty. They are lovers.

The real reason she's swearing is that they're on their way to an evening art party. He knows how they make her feel. The art parties they attend together are full of false-ness. He is a white male genius artist in San Francisco, and there is nothing real about white male genius artists in San Francisco: not the art, not the women who live with them, not the men who live with them, not the galleries, not the critics—*My god, the art critics, can't we just shoot them?*—not even San Francisco. Everything is filmy, filmy as bay fog.

All of them together make one big pile of shit, she de-clares, grabbing his hand as they approach the neighbor-hood of this evening's party. He squeezes her hand. She squeezes back, thinking, *How meaningless*, wondering, *Where is the risk in squeezing a lover's hand while walking to an art party?*

They pass rows of colored houses, staring forward like so many faces. Her descriptions: the fucking amazing view, the goddamn little rows of windows stretching for fucking miles. His: more azure evening light, warm glow from the inside out, houses alive. Doors, windows, roofs speaking. They make a good pair, or rather their mouths do: hers pushing out, exploding, his soaking everything in, slow and sweet.

When they're almost there, she suggests, wild, Why don't they run back down the hill, past the doors and windows and faces into the evening. She starts to unbutton her blouse. The light is dim; he can barely see her. She tugs at his arm, and he half believes her, as always. But just then someone sees him from the party house and calls out his name, so they turn around and go in after all. She leaves her excitement standing in the yard, leaning toward the night, eyes wide, chest heaving, naked.

INSIDE, EVERYONE CALLS him Pater. His name is Peter, she corrects them, but she is the only one who calls him this. Finally some man with a mostly bald head except for some styled and sculpted gray on the sides explains to her that Pater sounds more like the name of an artist, that more people will buy from a Pater than a Peter. She is astounded that he thinks he must tell her this. The paintings: What is being bought? Sometimes she can't remember his name at all, simply his paintings.

At the art party she does what angry women do. She

drinks. A lot. Language in the rooms of the party suddenly turns liquid. Animals begin crawling out. One man becomes a lizard, his belly scraping the shag carpet, his arms and legs sticking out stiff from his body. Another man who has been pinching the asses of women all night turns into a crab with one huge red claw, so heavy he cannot lift it anymore. A woman with big lips becomes a blowfish, bubbles rising from her face now and then; her eyes, moved to the sides of her head, look magnified. Peter, Pater, becomes a bird with extravagant colored plumage, terribly magnificent: His back sways, his chest protrudes.

She drinks wine she drinks whiskey she drinks beer she drinks tequila shots. She still feels like a fucking person. She goes into the bathroom and removes her bra and underwear from beneath her clothing and stuffs them into the medicine cabinet. She emerges from the bathroom some new animal that no one has ever seen before. Everyone notices her. She pretends they all see her as a magnificent exploding poppy but knows they likely see her as a stain. In her head she names herself something between the color red and the word "devour." She looks for him.

Some small man who might be a ferret or a weasel is talking to Pater/Peter, the rooster or the peacock. Everything swims. She watches her lover shrink. She moves closer. The ferret/weasel's mouth is making sharp, jerky movements. Closer still she hears words like "ridiculous" and "no talent" and "not a chance in hell." Her lover is shrinking before the weasel into a small bird, then into a chick, peeping uselessly. The ferret-man's tongue looks long and dangerous; his lips are knives moving together, slicing and clicking.

She hates. She hates the ferret, she hates the smallness of the chick. She hates the alcohol, she hates the art party, the animals, the body who came into the house. The ferret's mouth becomes the only thing she can focus on, even as a crowd is gathering—because by now of course she has started swearing, a mighty swear swarm, like starlings murmuring. Even as the fish-woman swims up and blows diplomatic bubbles between them, even as the giant red pincher drags itself near, the ferret's mouth clicks and slices and becomes more clear than is possible, so that finally she has a direction for her hate to aim at, and she punches his mouth right off his face. Everyone is a person again, humanly stunned.

A man rests on the floor. Her knuckles ache. Some quiet hands lead her away, a man whose name she cannot remember. He is saying, *It's all right, it's all right*. She suddenly realizes this is how she feels every goddamn night of her fucking life. His hands are on her face, her shoulders; he tries to sculpt her back into being okay. Her own hands hang useless.

This love cannot live unless she fights him every day of her life. He paints, will paint. She aches for it all to be over: the years, the relationship, the waiting. She aches to summer over into a different life. She runs toward summer with no hands. All mouth. He will paint with or without her.

COSMOS

THE CITY'S DESTINATION SKY PLANETARIUM GAVE A laserlight show every Thursday and Friday night. The show included the music of Pink Floyd—*Dark Side of the Moon*—and the audience was mostly teenagers. On these nights the planetarium lost its scientific propriety and gave way to sweat and to the movement of hands and lips sunk down low in theater seats. Constellations and galaxies surrendered to configurations of neon-colored light, geometric patterns translated into math equations. Music that failed to narrate and yet fully described. The eyes below did not study, just looked on stoned, glassy gray, and marble-like, filling the dome as close to full as was possible.

The planetarium had to be thoroughly cleaned every

Saturday morning, as the teenagers left all manner of themselves behind, like sticky and worn cultural artifacts. Food, gum, cigarette butts. Condoms and rolling papers. Lip gloss and rubber bands. Plastic drink containers, soda cans, straws, and beer bottles that rolled to the center of the floor and rested there like tiny spaceships, marooned and abandoned.

Ty Conner did the cleaning and had been doing so for the last eight years. He'd learned the species in precise detail, watched them gather there in the dark, recorded their behaviors, kept notes, formed hypotheses. His fascination with social organization and human structure filled his head with bubbles of untamed thought. The teens seemed to carry a world of matter and energy within them. Everything they left behind became something he wanted to save, to sort and arrange into a new thing that was beautiful and true. He wanted to harness and remake their entire existence.

Over time, from the materials they left behind, Ty had built in his home a kind of tiny city, an architecture of their leaving. He commandeered his dining room table and used it as a tableau of their existence, assembling the evidence of teen presence there like a sophisticated model of urban life.

It had started simply enough. He'd found a lipstick and brought it home, mesmerized by the mechanism, its easy

rise and fall reminding him of gears or pistons. He'd pictured it immediately as some kind of tower in a building
blueprint, not unlike smokestacks from the past, but in
this newer, futuresque city it would pump up and down
hydraulically, perhaps as a form of energy generation, perhaps as a mode of transport, similar to an elevator but more
advanced. That had been the first piece, leading to his first
drawings, and inspiring him to collect other objects, more
and more of them, each with a distinctive purpose in this
new city born of youth.

The teens who swarmed out of the planetarium left
things there that they didn't need or want, things that just
fell away from them like artifacts: a cracked iPhone, vari-
ous vape devices, batteries and atomizers, flasks and old-
school silver lighters, hair ties, a Fujifilm Instax Mini 9 in
bubble-gum pink, a wireless mobile Bluetooth speaker, a
pair of Beats headphones, all manner of water bottles, a
worn PS4 controller, a paracord bracelet. When he thought
about the objects and the city evolving from them, he was
filled with awe; he saw the future bright and beautiful, a
future that easily discarded morality and good citizenship
in favor of an existence based on liminality and provisional
presence, like television waves or information traveling by
phone wire or electromagnetic light. It all made perfect
sense to him: These beings left traces of themselves in the
objects they left behind, they represented a new order of

existence, new cultures and superstructures, space travel and cosmic weaponry fanning out into the cosmos. The vacant look in their eyes was not boredom or some residue of millennial apathy. It was the future dulling over ordinary vision. It was the past disappearing like discarded refuse.

No manner of event could draw him away from his obsession. By day he cleaned and at night he worked on the city. Saturday evenings were a watershed of knowledge and a plethora of work: minute, painstaking labor that involved the careful consideration of objects, the fierce action of the imagination, steady hands, and the will to create something from nothing. A bridge crossed a toxic-waste site through a series of elevated tunnels made from cans and paper. Cans of Coke and Sprite and Diet Pepsi connected buildings like commercial passageways. Condoms stretched taut between ballpoint pens created great tents over business and technology centers. The tents had a dual purpose: to house the work within a steady, temperature-controlled environment and to filter greenhouse gases through a complex biochemical procedure into hydrogen-oxygenated by-products, stored in heavy tanks made from water bottles.

One feature he was especially proud of was the garbage ventilation system, by which all manner of waste was sucked down to the underneath of the city and processed into usable fuels. Every social space had great vents at its edges, and all airborne or material pollutants were simply sucked away, three times daily, eliminating trash, pollution, even insects and rodents. After a terrible accident the first year of the program, grates had been installed to prevent small pets and children from being accidentally removed from the socius. Since then the city had only increased in efficiency and beauty. Ty had filled notebook after notebook with drawings and plans detailing systems such as these; sometimes, just before sleep, he imagined historians of the future discovering his notebooks and marveling at his foresight.

Amid these emotions, this daily activity, it happened one Saturday morning that Ty reached down under one of the Destination Sky Planetarium seats with his plastic-gloved hand and found himself holding an arm. At first he thought it was a baguette, like the one he'd found once before along with some molding brie and an empty wine bottle. Then he thought it might be some kind of gag: a summer sausage, a stuffed piece of pantyhose, something. But it was a human arm. Bodiless. The hand intact, stiff and clawing and white. His breath jackknifed in his lungs and his eyes bulged in their sockets and his mind raced: *What what what the fuck?* And even as he held the lifeless thing in his own plastic-covered hand, he couldn't get his brain to contain it, to lock on to it in the normal way. He just stood there like a great thick stuffed beast, unable to move or speak or stop looking at it gesturing at him. The arm was stiff and heavy, and his own arm and hand began to stiffen and grow heavy too, as when a limb goes to sleep or the brain forgets its body.

Some part of his mind, far away from conscious thought, had a long conversation about turning the arm in to the authorities, but instead he found himself putting it in the bag he saved for objects to take home with him. He spent the rest of the day in an awkward, herky-jerky daze. He spilled chlorine bleach over the seats in the front row, and the smell of a swimming pool on overload filled the dome, nauseating, a hard ice pick to the temple.

That night he did not work on his city at all. Instead he walked to the part of town where the local kids hung out, until his eye was caught by a teen couple across the street—a boy and a girl, or a man and a woman still becoming. He stopped and pretended to pick up a bit of trash as they entered a coffee shop, the hipster kind with a floor-to-ceiling window in front. He walked over to the nearest trash receptacle and lingered there, watching them. A bunch of teens hanging out together wouldn't notice a man across the street. He could be a vagrant. He could be anyone. He was as close to being invisible as possible.

What he saw as he watched made his chest ache. The boy put his hand on the girl's hand. The girl kept looking down at the table and smiling. The boy wiped his hands on his pants—once, then twice, the damp heat of youth. They were beautiful. They were terrible.

His elbow ached; his arm had gone a little numb from leaning on the trash bin. He could feel the sting of tears and that walnut in the throat when you're trying not to cry.

The one and only time he'd asked a woman to a movie, she had an asthma attack in the middle of the film. An ambulance came. He thought she might die. He thought it would be his fault. He never contacted her again. That's what you get for thinking you get to be in the world like other mammals, he decided. He unwrapped a ball of throat lozenge wrappers—they had fallen from her pocket as they hoisted her stretcher—and made them part of his city. A crown of golden cellophane light atop a skyscraper made of toilet paper rolls. Then he drank three-quarters of a bottle of Jack Daniel's and fell asleep on the living room floor, the thick shag carpet tickling the edges of his ears and fingers.

In the night, strange visions made a fist of his brain, twisting his thoughts toward his greatest challenge. His city was inorganic, artificial in every sense. He'd been ignoring the fact of it, having taken such joy in the world of objects and design. Surfaces. He'd made no attempt to render nature: no miniature trees, water, dirt, worms, rot, or any of the elements that make up a world. He'd concentrated solely on the artificial, the built environment, and the science required to hold it up. The arm entered his dreams not as an arm but as an argument, as a logic of the organic and the biological. The arm had a mouth and spoke to him clearly. *There is no life without death*, the arm said, *organic and perfect*. In the middle of the night he woke and added some bleach to the whiskey, a little cocktail. His lips puckered and burned. A sore formed quickly in his mouth. He vomited, his throat on fire, and fell back to the floor.

When he awoke late the next morning, he had not a hangover but a clarity of vision as sharp as a diamond lodged in the center of a skull. He understood with full force the error he had made, with his little city on the table, with his lack of drive, with his life. He saw with bright white light that his entire existence had been leading up to a single moment, that he'd very nearly blinked and missed it, the way we often do in our lives, droning along in what's ordinary and familiar, missing the moment at hand even when everything in the universe is pointing the way toward sight. He saw that his superficial efforts with refuse were the key, that *decay itself* was the giver of life, the secret of the universe, the place from which all stars collapse and all systems tower and all logic gets born and then falls.

He'd simply mistaken the act for the thing itself.

He stared at the darkening, shrivel-skinned arm. He poured himself another cocktail and drank. Still coughing, he headed back to his city, thinking of all the death it takes for life to flourish.

He laid himself down on the dining room table along-side the new city, his arm next to the dead one, and thought of all the teenagers in the Destination Sky Planetarium, seething and coupling, and he cradled the arm, slightly blue and stiff, in the crux of his own, and he closed his eyes to the world and readied himself, not for sleep but for alchemy—for the shifting of molecules, the transmutation from solid to another form, from metal to gold, or liquid, or the speed of light itself.

SECOND LANGUAGE

SOMETIMES SHE UNDERSTOOD HERSELF, IN THIS new place, as a body inside out. A body no longer contained, leaking meanings. She tucked in the corners of her face and went back out into the world, knowing that the bloodstreaks in the street behind her would repulse at least some bystanders.

The blue veins standing out in her neck and at her temples made her look eerily like a map of Siberia. Even though in this place she knew that the word "Siberia" did not signify, somehow she took comfort in the Siberian look of her neck and temple veins; just thinking of it made her walk with a slightly straighter spine, a girl of the North. Though some people she passed looked at her with a kind of disaffected latte pity, it made a lot of sense to her. Her mother, grandmother, and great-grandmother had been Lithuanian, had survived winters, had been sold to Russians, had died in white and cold and poverty, and so a vast white expanse with rivulets of black and blue was a concept she understood. Didn't land look that way to birds on great journeys? Birds had outlived the Ice Age. Perhaps my body is like a place seen from the sky, she thought. She looked up. Then she returned her gaze to the faces of this American city.

She had a vague understanding that her insides were visible on the outside—and how unfamiliar that appeared—but what were exposed capillaries and dangling entrails compared to the wallets of businessmen jutting from the asses of their fine suits, or the violently painted lips of women whose hairstyles and manicures rivaled their mortgage payments?

She looked up. Gray sky, gray buildings. Concrete with wind. At least there were trees here. Trees never lie. But where in the world, she wondered, were the graywolves?

Pulsing outward, she made her way to the front man whose address she'd been given when she arrived, after crossing over from Canada in a white-painted popsicle truck. Girls like popsicles driven over stitched borders between nations. Apparently this kind of front man did not regard an inside-out girl as unusual or damaged. "Are you at least a C cup?" the man on the phone had asked. She still had her use value in this place, is what she understood him to mean. Her heart hidden behind the new pillows of her adolescence.

The front man lived near a freeway—what freedom was it meant to have?—in a snot-colored two-story house with black plastic in the windows where curtains should be. When she knocked on the door, her throat cords braided and her vertebrae clattered. The man who answered the door looked to be in his late teens. Older than her. Inside were more girl popsicles, most of them around twelve or thirteen by the look of it. One might have been fourteen, but height wasn't necessarily a sign of age. At least two of them looked young enough to need mothers. She stared at the melting popsicles, her kin, all of them with too-thin, too-white wrists wound with bulging blue rivulets. But the television in the living room bombarded her senses with image and sound in waves. She bit down on her tongue enough to feel it.

Good blood in a mouth. A warm that delivers you, that returns you.

Days went by, enough to create time.

She ate.

Slept.

And in the evenings, every evening, she was delivered to some new address.

Each address had an old gray man billionaire with money enough for a girl's body and threat enough to take her life.

The pretend pretty of the Portland city all around her days: disposable cartons and plastic and paper and coffee-coffeecoffee and black clothes and bike lanes and funny little hats and eating and driving and thousands of kinds of potato chips. Whole aisles at grocery stores devoted to potato chips, salty ones and square ones, greenblueyellowred ones, chips with pepper and chips with vinegar and some with "bar b q" flavor, red with salty dye. Coffee spilling from the mouths of hundreds of shops and beerbeerbeer everywhere and strip clubs outnumbering McDonald's. She wondered if all these regular well-dressed people walking around like Bic lighters had been to the strip clubs or if she was the only one. If they did go, were they the same after? Her emotional circuitry was interrupted every time she took off her clothes.

Of the land in this Portland, there were mountains, and she remembered that terrain could still overtake human lives. She wished she could hear their stories, but she couldn't from where she was, boxed here.

She saw the lively mouths and freshly sculpted bodies and the surface sheen of the people in this city, she saw their righteous bicycling circles and their coffee corners and the neon signage and the stutter of bridges over incarcerated rivers. Still, even walking the sidewalks, smelling the pee and rotting food mixed with car exhaust and wet leaves and dirt, she could see that money and consumption were what the place was made of. Everyone seemed to be worth so much. How did they wear their *I*'s so easily?

Sometimes while walking, she witnessed animal behavior: blue jays adopting different languages, gardener snakes S-gliding over concrete into their shrub havens. The cacophony of frogs under overpasses near streams or gutters. Walking nowhere reflected back to her a sense of non-being she could live with. Sometimes she stopped to sit in the dirt, and an old beer would tumble by. Coors, it said.

She considered trying to speak to other mammals. But her voice locked in her throat when she thought of what she was: a girl with nothing, no money, no family, a name without documents. All she could feel was the warm cave between her legs and the small and sure soft swell of each of her breasts. Well, at least my body has meaning, she thought. Value signifies meaning, right?

In the evenings, when she was delivered like a cardboard box from a UPS truck, sifted through by rummaging hands like recycling, she went dead.

Her nightly destinations threatened to unweave her intestines and pour them out in a gray mucous line onto the street. Somewhere in her skull or rib cage, the hint of old ideas—family, home—lingered, but the memories were not strong enough to negate their absence in this place. In this place her being was her bodyworth. In this place it was be or die.

This night, like every other, the doorway to the hotel looked to her like the yawning mouth of an old man. Repetition makes a thing real. The everynight of things entering a body until a path was carved.

Her eyeballs shivered, and her rib cage made a sound in the wind like chimes. Knocking on the door took more than a girl.

Well, she thought, even if I am entering the loose-skinned mouth of a saggy old man, *a job's a job*. A phrase she'd lifted from the mouths of other popsicles as a survival mantra. Along with this: Do not do not do not behave "like an immigrant." Do not out yourself. Language is a funny thing, she thought. It opens and closes. It trips you like a crack in the sidewalk. Keep moving or die.

On the television in the hotel bedroom of the slackened old gray man—her john for the evening—was a war zone. Between the old gray john's legs she could see the televised rubble, the huddled clumps of human crouched and lurching and running. "Suck," he said. Deflated bad-tasting balloons filled the wet opening of her mouth. The rubble and the humans and the CNN ticker tape . . . she closed her eyes and sucked. He fingered into her. He put his jowls down near her face, his mouth to her ear: "I'm a very important man . . . *the most important* man. . . . Your little holes are so tight." He smiled wide enough for her to see the pink of his receding gums.

There was one thing besides her body that she possessed—a story, in a foreign tongue but still a story—and always upon her return to the front man's concrete house she would relate the story to the other popsicles. She did not know why she retold it, only that the recitation could not be stopped. What else did she have? What currency but story? Like the continual expulsion of her insides to the outside, story came. And the popsicles would lean in, eyes wide, mouths and wrists open to the future, and listen.

Long ago in a faraway land, there was a czar who had a magnificent orchard, an orchard second to none. However, every night a firebird would swoop down on the czar's best apple tree and fly away with a few golden apples. The czar ordered each of his three sons to catch that firebird alive and bring it to him.

The two elder brothers fell asleep while watching. The youngest son, Ivan, saw the firebird and grabbed it by the tail, but the bird managed to wriggle out of Ivan's grasp, leaving him only a bright red tail feather.

Ivan, assisted by a graywolf who killed his horse and then felt sorry for him, because even wolves understand how unfortunate men are, managed to get not only the firebird but also a wonderful horse and a princess named Elena the Fair. When they came to the border of Ivan's father's kingdom, Ivan and Elena stopped to rest. While they were sleeping, Ivan's two older brothers, returning from their unsuccessful quest, came across the two and killed Ivan, threatening Elena to do the same to her if she told what had happened. They ravaged Elena and threatened to cut out her tongue.

Ivan lay dead for thirty days until the graywolf revived him with water of death and water of life. Ivan came to his home palace at the wedding day of Elena the Fair and one of Ivan's brothers. The czar asked for an explanation, and Elena, with the wolf standing guard gnashing his teeth, told him the truth. The czar was furious and threw the elder brothers into prison. The wolf ate their entrails out in the night. Ivan and Elena the Fair married, inherited the kingdom, and lived happily ever after.

None of the popsicles ever said a word about the story. But her telling brought sleep lapping over them like a kind night ritual.

TIME PASSED. Enough for her to realize no graywolves would come.

Although she knew that stories had beginnings, middles, and ends, she also knew that, for her and those displaced like her, the order was out of whack. Once story had been like home, but now story had been fragmented and gnawed at the edges. Once there were heroes and saviors, but they had turned into con artists and reality-TV stars and dizzy whirring consumers. Or maybe there had never been any heroes and saviors and those stories were only meant to trick girls into forgetting how to be animals.

Just as it lengthened her spine, strength in a girl like her made her eyes smaller and steelier, her jaw more square, her cheekbones high like canted clamshells. Even her collarbone spoke, but in this place people didn't seem to hear. They responded with dead stares or shrugged shoulders.

You need to speak better English, they said.

She longed for the graywolves, furred and growling and teethed, to rip loose the entrails of enemies.

The last night, in the hours before dawn, after she was delivered back to the house of ravaged popsicles, after she had again told the story from her mother dead, her grandmother dead, her great-grandmother dead, after she had washed the blood from her mouth, her nipples, from between her legs where she realized life would never pass the way it had moved from the cleft of her mother, her grandmother, her great-grandmother, and the blood from the smaller aperture of her ass, the rivulets of red winding their way down the rusted drain holes of an unclean shower, when she put herself down on a formless mattress on the floor under a window of the house filled with girl popsicles, the cave of her concrete world opened up—cracks in

reality—and through the window she could see the tower-
ing white-eyed angels hovering over them, streetlights,
they called them here, and a nightwatch of lost leaves whispered against her hair. Tin and paper rustlings made urban
lullabies. Or maybe it was just the ugly end of the city, like
everyone kept saying on television, where girls go to disap-
pear and die. She wondered if death could transform into
an animal, by her own hand even. Not as an ending but as
a bluewhitened pulsar; couldn't it, blazing the entire night
sky apart and atomizing everything ever done to girls?
Couldn't deranged graywolves come back from old stories,
from native land, to tear out the throats and sagging balls of
old gray johns; couldn't they enter through astral projections ancient as folktales embedded in the dead bones of
her mother and hers and hers, gone to dirt but still alive
there—charged? Weren't there still secret triumphs, secret
powers, to living dead girls?

There were; she could feel it. The strength that lived in
this popsicle house. She could feel it, and she had no word
for it.

Without thinking, she punched a hole with her fist
through the window in their cinder-block box. She elbowed
the hole until it was big enough for the popsicles to leave,
elbow blood everywhere; then, quiet as a mother's voice
singing a child to sleep in a mothertongue, they slipped
out. As the popsicles tumbled out into the night like child

refugees—oh! how they glowed like human snowflakes underneath the streetlights!—she knew what else to do. She'd have to conjure the graywolves. Not the old gray wrong American manwolves, but the real thing.

She took the broken pieces of window glass and gutted herself so that her entrails were finally fully free and right. They slithered out in vivid shades of girl onto the floor. Someone must stay behind to help the dream come true.

And it did, for only then did the real graywolves smell it—her entrails, animal and good—and they came down from the mountains one, two, three, four, ten, twenty, and entered the cinder-block house and ripped the throats from the wrongheaded men and tore them limb from limb, and the wolves' teeth and howls reminded everyone everywhere how there is something from spine and ice that has yet to form a language, a yet-unfinished sentence, one those bought-and-sold Eastern European girls are learning besides English: They are learning to gut themselves open so that others will run.

I tell you, do not go near that place. Do not go near it. Graywolves guard the ground there. Girls are growing from guts, enough for a body and a language all the way out of this world.

A WOMAN
SIGNIFYING

YOU DON'T SEE CAST-IRON RADIATORS MUCH ANY-more, the old-fashioned kind. People have learned to be careful around them. But her building was old. She stared at the radiator's vertical lines and thought about old obsolete things. She took a deep breath, then touched her cheek to the radiator for three long seconds. It was a perfectly calm gesture, seemingly disaffected but deliberate all the same. "One, two, three," she said, breathing out with each word. One, two three: The heat singed silent through the layers of her skin, through the fleshy part of her cheek.

When she had finally thought of it, how proud she'd been. It had happened in the time it takes to scald a wrist cooking bacon. They'd been standing in the kitchen, she'd been making them breakfast, he'd said, "I'll be working late again tonight, don't wait up for me," and she could feel her own ass sag, her love handles bulge, her chin develop a double; she could feel their sexlessness making mounds of her body like biscuits.

What patience she had! What brave, glorious, undaunted patience. And even then she had realized it would *take* patience—patience to sit in front of the hot metal, patience to draw her face near, and nearer even as the heat became evident, whispering toward her cheek. Patience at the moment itself, to do it right, to pull away slowly, for after all she did not want to rip half her face off and leave it staring back at her from the radiator. She wanted a controlled effort, a specific result. Only a wound, a perfect wound. She was absolutely confident at the idea, because what was this patience compared to her life? Three small seconds.

She winced or smiled as she peeled her cheek away. Burned, sweet flesh tickled her nostrils. Her eyes welled, swam in their little sockets. When she could see properly again, she rose and staggered, flesh screaming, from the living room to the kitchen.

The first thing she did was pour herself a glass of vodka. The kind of glass one might fill with milk. She drank it down until the heat in her throat and chest challenged the fire in her right cheek, the fire filling the right side of her face now, making her nostril flare a bit, her lip quiver, her eye close. The vodka streamed down the center of her body, a streak of high voltage.

She thought of things her women friends had said to her over their scripted lunches: consolation, advice, admonishment. Come on, be serious, get a grip. You don't really hate him, do you? Grow up! Be sensible, have some self-control. Maybe go on a diet—herbs and tofu. You'll feel better. Change your hair. Your perfume. Your heels. Make something of your life. Sex isn't everything, don't be ridiculous. You are obsessing. You are playing the victim. You're just being lazy. I wish I had your problem!

Or: Honey, what you need is a good fuck.

How do you tell women who wear fake nails and baby powder between their legs and order chicken salads with vinaigrette at linen-covered tables and try desperately to chew without smudging their lipstick that women must keep moving or die?

She walked around her living room holding her drink, feeling animated. Alive. Gesturing with her drink to the TV, the couch, the different objects in the room, yelling at everything and nothing.

"He's not the only one who can play this game!" she shouted, confronting a lamp. "Fucker! Motherfucker!" She trudged back and forth across the carpet. "I hate you! I hate you! I've given you half of my life, you fucking bastard!" She brought the glass of vodka up to her mouth so hard it clanged against her teeth.

What advice was there for a woman's epic anger when it

was equaled in intensity only by need? The room swelled with shame and silence.

The now-cold pain in her cheek pierced straight through her skull. She thought maybe her right eye had swollen shut, or at any rate she could no longer open it. She went to the bathroom to have a look. On her way she realized this was all a little disgusting, the kind of story that would make the listener lean a little away from her. *Not in public. Not so close.* "Should we keep quiet?" she whispered to the bathroom door. "See where keeping quiet has gotten us." Then she opened it and looked herself in the face.

That really is a beauty, she thought. The outer edge was deep red and crimped; a purplish welt rose on either side like mangled lips. In the center of that, a long, yellowish bubble of blistered skin like sea foam. An amazing wound. A well-thought-out, carefully executed wound. Kind of perfect.

By the time he gets home, she'll be out already. By the time he gets home, she'll have outlined her own eyes in black, added lashes in blue. By the time he gets home, she'll be blushed and lipsticked, red as a Coca-Cola can. Push-up bra and Spanx. By the time he gets home, after she's stared at the tools of the face for a long while, she'll have decided on a gold-dust shadow, she'll have traced a gleaming glow around the thing, ringed it in precious metal. By the time he gets home, she'll be sitting in a bar with the most perfect wound imaginable. A symbol of it all, her face the word for it.

THE ELEVENTH
COMMANDMENT

TO THIS DAY I DON'T KNOW WHY SHE HUNG OUT with me. I was pitiful. Sickly, pale, booger-picking. Braces. Matted hair that argued with itself like crazy. The works. You can imagine: I was the kid who sat in those concrete tunnels by myself all during recess, who wet my pants during social studies in sixth grade. You heard right. Sixth grade. I had already developed several neuroses. I had the stress of a forty-eight-year-old man. Are you getting the picture? Sure you are. Everyone knew a kid like me.

The first time I met her, she came into one of those tunnels and sat down next to me without saying a word. For the whole recess. I didn't say a word either. I was scared, but also weirdly thankful. She didn't even look at me.

The next day she got in there with me again. Finally, toward the end of the forty-five minutes, she said, Chris Backstrom has hair around his pecker. That's all. Then the bell rang and she ran out, and I sat there for a while longer considering this. Chris Backstrom had blond hair, so I tried to picture blond hair growing in beautiful curls around his penis. I shuddered and thought I might vomit. Then I got a splitting headache. I kept checking to see if my nose was bleeding. By the time I made it back to the classroom, I was near fainting with pain, and they sent me to the nurse's office. After some time my mother picked me up, and I went home. She was very angry.

About a week later, the girl came back down and said she wanted to show me something. She said it was very important and that never in a million years would I get the chance again. Then she asked me if I wanted to see. My mouth was filled with saliva, and my palms were sweaty. I felt an uncontrollable urge to pick my nose; then I thought I might have to pee. I said yes in a wobbly little voice. I thought I might have gone cross-eyed there for a second.

She lifted up her skirt, and she pulled her panties down. This smell filled the concrete tunnel, and it was good but it was also terrifying, and I thought I could somehow taste it.

When I look back, I think of how she saved my life that day.

Her pussy had little red hairs on it, and she said, See,

this is very rare. And she took my hand and we petted her together.

Later she coaxed me out of the tunnel, and we walked around to the far end of the field where the goalposts were. Some boys were playing soccer, and true as life the ball ended up clocking me upside the head. My face turned redder than humanly possible; I thought my skull might burst like an overripe fruit. I pictured it exploding there on the field, pictured how everyone would laugh, then stop and stare, stunned, confronting the death laid bare before them, the dull head of a boy in pieces at their feet.

The boys came toward us, and then I pictured another death, death by pulverization, death by soccer players cannibalizing me on the field. Food, I felt like: too-white food.

As always in grade school, they started to taunt me, ignoring her but drawing a tight circle around me until it felt like the oxygen was being sucked right out of my lungs. One of the leaders of the pack came up and stood over me, his chest puffing out, his great mouth opening and closing, his teeth drawing nearer, yelling and spraying spit, his breath hot and burning on my face. Finally his hand drew back and his body moved on me with the weight of an animal.

Then suddenly she was there, between us, stopping the turning of the world. She said, You know about the Eleventh Commandment, don't you?

The guy tried to shove her aside, but she shouldered her way back in; she was taller than him, as is often the case at that age.

The Eleventh Commandment, she said again. It's in this secret book that someone found in a clay pot. They kept all the secret stuff out of the real Bible because it scared people too much and it was too difficult for most people to understand. You had to have intelligence, but you also had to have imagination, and most people barely have the one and none of the other. Like you chuckleheads.

Baffled by this development, the gang of soccer players let the insult pass.

In the secret book there is an extra commandment, she went on, and it's bigger and more serious than all the other ones, because it includes what will happen to you if you sin against it. Some boy to the side yelled out, You're full of shit, there's only one Bible, shut up you stupid bitch! She headed over to him, still talking, until her words were breath-close to his face. The reason you don't know about it, dumbfuck, is that no one thinks you're smart enough to get it. They don't let just anyone in on it. You have to prove yourself. You have to show them you're worthy, mature, that you can handle it. But I'm gonna tell you because you're all too stupid to get that far, and I think it might save you some trouble later in life.

I don't know how girls like that get the power to lead

people. I don't know what it was about her—she wasn't pretty like the popular girls, and she wasn't athletic either. It was more like she had this tiny bit of craziness that made people scared of her, but, like all disruption, it made you want to look, listen.

Some other schmuck called out, Well, how the hell did *you* hear about it, then?

Mary Shelley came to me in a dream and told me about it, she replied calmly.

Who the hell is that? the same guy said.

She took a deep breath and said, Mary Shelley, shit-for-brains, wrote *Frankenstein*, the greatest book of all time. If any of you idiots knew how to fucking read, you'd know that.

Then she made her way back over to me—me standing in a puddle of fear, airless, weightless, dizzy, already having surrendered, already having left my body to take my beating and accept it. Then, standing near me, she told the story of the Eleventh Commandment.

There was this leper, she said, who was friends with Jesus. Everybody was grossed out by him on account of his nastiness—his skin was all gray and full of pus, and he had these horrible open wounds and shit. He was actually a pretty nice guy, but no one wanted to go near him, and since most humans are ignorant, they translated their disgust of his skin to *him*, deciding he was dangerous, deviant, and evil. But Jesus, being smart, really liked him. He even thought the skin thing was interesting—after all, the man's suffering made him closer to God. Besides, Jesus had played chess and drunk and had great philosophical conversations with him, so he knew he was dope. It was just the town losers, who didn't know shit, who hated him.

So one day this kid passed by the leper's house and peeked inside the window and saw the leper and Jesus fucking. (At this point the crowd of boys began to hurl obscenities at her in disbelief.) I know, she went on, the town reacted exactly like you morons. But the fact was, Jesus and the leper were fucking. So the town, like you *assholes*, decided that Jesus was possessed by the leper-devil, that he was under some kind of leper-devil hex, and they set out to save him.

They were stupid, so their plan was stupid. They decided to wait for the leper to go to sleep and then burn him and his house to ash. But of course Jesus ended up in bed with the leper that night, and those idiots burned 'em both to ash.

Well, God was pretty pissed, as you can imagine. The next morning he cracked the sky open with lightning and put out the eye of the sun and threw down a rock slab bearing a new commandment. Thou shalt for the rest of time be stricken with disease, it said, when thou settest eyes upon the uncanny.

The minute they read that thing, all their dicks turned black and the pain of acid on flesh shriveled them up, and after a week or so their peckers dropped off altogether. And that's what happens to anyone who rejects the uncanny without wondering what it means, without recognizing that they're looking at a fucking miracle.

It was the strangest story we'd ever heard—strange because we didn't know what "uncanny" meant, but also because she did, and because our little dicks were getting hard from this tall girl telling it to us. Strange because we hated anything about homos, because that's what people called us when they wanted to beat us up, and strange because half of us were, or were on our way to becoming, what those beat-us-up boys hated—bodies that felt like home.

It's not like they couldn't have beaten the crap out of my sorry ass anyhow, or pushed her around, or played out their sadism in any number of other ways. But somehow by the end of her story, a little path leading off the field had cleared for us, and she walked it, and I followed her, and I got the impression that the waves would hold like that until the Romans turned to chase us, at which point they would be consumed by the sea, or perhaps just by all of their ignorance drowning them and washing them away.

DRIVE
THROUGH

IN YOUR CAR. YOUR RED TOYOTA COROLLA. EXHAUST
hums in front of you, behind you. Small voices scratch out
of giant boxes with writing on them. Drivers dig through
pockets, ready their money. The sun dips down into her
wallow; evening descends on a line of cars in the drive-
thru at McDonald's.

A tiny man in the distance. You can see him in the rearview, just above the words OBJECTS IN MIRROR ARE CLOSER
THAN THEY APPEAR. He is on the move, window to window,
car to car. In the rearview you can see the faces of other
drivers pinch up as he nears their cars. They dread him.
Already they are cringing, scrunching up their shoulders,
locking their doors, working buttonholes with their asses

in the vinyl seats, trying desperately to look at something else. Anything but the approaching man, bearded, hair knotted, slightly dirty, clothes rumpled and clearly week-worn. White male, thirty-five, maybe forty-five.

By the time you get to the young black man in the first window, huge waves of relief send a shiver up your back. You've made it, goddammit, and an angel has appeared to take your money. There is no room for the nasty white man begging money to come around to your driver's-side window, he could never fit between the ledge of the window with the guardian angel and the safety of your car, your finger on the button to raise your window should danger appear. The young man takes your money and returns your change, asks you what kind of sauce you want, gives it to you in a beautiful little white bag with golden arches on it, why, it's heaven, it's just like being in heaven, the delight is filling your whole body now, earlier you thought you had to pee and the line of cars seemed unbearable, but now, now you are making an exchange that is simple and good and profound in its truth. The young man smiles and waves as you head slowly to the second window, his salary doesn't even enter your mind, you are free, you are on the way to the second window.

Surely he is at one of the cars behind you. Surely things will get held up there, someone will refuse to open their window and he will knock on it, or he will appear inside the frame of the front windshield and the driver will avert her gaze, he will give up and move on, or back, or away. You risk a quick look in your rearview—nothing nothing nothing, like pennies from heaven.

Your car glides almost magically to the second window, its opening apparent, hands visible, a bag of food bulging and white and smelling of good oil—all vegetable oil—and fried things. Your family is waiting at home. Your car is filled with gas. Your money has been paid.

A pimply-faced girl with headgear and braces hands you your bag, and you see capitalism and youth emerging from the window, you see her first summer job, her first lessons at responsibility and a savings account and taking care of herself, you see her on her way to college, yes, that's it, the summer before college, the lessons she is learning, what a good student she will make, how she will excel in school, how she will learn well, how she will enter the workforce with a good head on her shoulders. And then there is a rapping at your window on the passenger side, and strange how you forgot, isn't it? And your head swivels over out of dumb instinct, and there he is, his bad teeth and leathery skin and marble-blurred eyes filling the window, like a close-up, magnified, terrifying. His horrible mouth is opening and closing, he is saying something to you, he is talking to you, his muffled voice breaking through the glass shelter, now he is yelling, you are clutching your bag for dear life, you are putting your car in drive, his fingers at the ledge of your world, your own body like a snake's: all spine and nerve.

Then a new image: From the front window, you see a man in uniform, my God, an older man with a McDonald's uniform complete with cap and manager's badge is running toward your car, he is waving his arms, he is shouting. With one hand you are clutching your steering wheel as in a near-miss accident, and with the other hand you are clutching your white bag of food, heavy and full, and your eyes are like a frozen deer's, and your body is taut, and your nipples are hard as little stones. Your mouth is dry, and you are as alert as you are capable of being. The manager yells at the shitty little begging white man, You go now! You go now! You outta here now! Shithead! Motherfucking! You go! No slaving here! His slip of the tongue doesn't even faze you. You are with him. United. You are grateful. There is no dividing you. The two of you are in it together, you are saving each other, you are making the world a better place, you are the American way embodied, you are at each other's back, you are two hundred billion served.

CUSP

There is nowhere a girl can go. The only runaway
position is prostitution and that can kill you
about as fast as a violent uncle or a crazy daddy.

—*Dorothy Allison*

THIS BED SMELLS OF MY SKIN. IF I ROLL FROM MY
back to my belly, sweat cools near my spine. If I close my
eyes, I am like an animal up here in the heat and wood,
baking in the daylight, my eyelids heavy, my thoughts slow
and thudding. I am waiting for dark, for the release, for
breathing to animate me. This room and everything in it
brings me closer to myself: nocturnal.

From the frame of my attic window, I have imagined the
inside-out of this town. Its heat rising from dust and scrub,
its mindless longing for rain, its heart beating with dumb

insistence. Outside my room the world has expanded and contracted like the tight little fist of a child. Years have gone by. I used to wonder who would want to live here, like this, some dried-out town at the edge of the story line, the nightly news, never quite making it into the picture, its people crowding the geography somehow without evolution or design. There is a black-and-red sign over the door of the Texaco. It reads TEXAS, USA. No city. No need. That's the whole deal, stuck up there on a piece of metal the size of a license plate. Like thought stopped for gas and died at the pump.

I remember the day I moved from my room downstairs up to the attic. It had been my brother's. He'd gone to college, I'd hit puberty, the two motions crackling away from each other like electrical currents. The white canopy bed of a girl died that day, for I never went back. The day I moved into my brother's attic room, I felt the wooden walls close in around me, as if a second body were there to hold me. The wood grain looked to me like dark, warm skin, comforting me.

Underneath the bed I found artifacts from my brother's life. Empty bottles and broken glass, trash, foil, used rubbers and tissues, tiny vials and a stretch of surgical tubing. It was a year before I found any needles, but it wasn't for lack of trying. He'd shown me his world when I was around ten, knowing I would love it as I loved every moment he let me be in his attic, adoring him, adoring the dark of the room, the broken rules, the thick unbearable silence, the smells I hadn't names for, the dizzy swell of skin making sweat. But I did find everything. A loose board in the wall, a stash I only barely comprehended at the time. Wasn't I meant to find it, to find it all? Wasn't I meant to identify the smell as sex and move my body toward delivering itself? Wasn't I meant to prove my worth, to carry on the weight of that room?

On my fourteenth birthday, I got a bottle of Jack Daniel's from my brother. He was home from college for the summer. He gave it to me in secret, after dark, and we sat up in the attic window that connected our lives and drank it until I was bleary and swollen and unable to focus. At some point after midnight, we became overheated and half clothed. The heat works on you like that. You shed layers like the skin of a snake until the body can bear itself. My brother brought the whiskey to his face, took it, held it in his mouth like that with his eyes closed.

"Well," he said, "it's almost here, huh?"

"You mean that?" I asked, pointing out the window toward the future, toward the place out in the dark where they were building. It was a prison, or the idea of one, a place of curiosity and danger emerging in the town that was smothering us.

"Yeah, guess that will change things around here."

"It's the best thing that's ever happened to me in my sorry-ass little life."

He looked at me, I think he toasted me, and he said, "You'll get out soon enough. You'll see. When you get out, it's a whole new world, a new life."

"What if I don't get out?"

He laughed and laughed. "You? You were out the day you were born. You'll probably end up at Harvard or some fancy shit. You've got brains."

"You've got brains too," I said. "That's how you got where you are." He snorted and downed his drink.

"Pour me another," and then, "You don't know what the fuck you're talking about."

"What do you mean?"

He looked at me a long time, as if he were judging what I could handle. Finally he took a new sip and said, "Between you and me?"

"Sure."

"I dropped out."

"What the hell are you talking about?"

"I quit. I haven't been back for months. I've been working at a construction site near my apartment and selling some shit on the side. It's not great, but it's a life. And I'm meeting people—important guys. Guys who are connected."

"Wait—you're telling everybody you're at college when in reality you're fucking *conning us*?"

"What's the con? I'm making a living on my own. I've got money. A job. Sex. Whatever I want. And like I said, I'm meeting some important people. The building we're working on right now is filled with money. It's a big opportunity. The guy behind the scenes is filthy rich. Had us up to his house in Dallas for a party. Wild, man. Chicks walking around with nothing but G-strings on, carrying mirrors of coke lines like platters at a restaurant. Pussy everywhere."

I looked down at my hands, then down into my own lap.

"What's the matter? Hasn't anyone ever said 'pussy' to you?"

I nodded but couldn't look up. My face was so hot I thought my head might explode. My hands made a pathetic cup between my legs.

He laughed again. "Don't worry, baby. You'll grow up soon enough." He poured me another. "The whole world is one big fuckfest. Forget this life. Forget families—mothers, fathers, schools, jobs. There are only two kinds of winning, two ways of keeping score: bucks and fucks."

I tried to laugh knowingly, then drank, then just sat there. I'll admit it, I was in awe. We sat in silence after that.

Then he handed me something wrapped in what looked like the brown paper of a liquor store bag. The paper crackled as I opened it. It was a flask: a gift.

That birthday, from my parents, I received a set of all of Shakespeare's tragedies, used copies, but beautiful somehow. The covers were dark red, with embossed lettering, and inside, the pages were as thin as moths' wings. I could picture them burning, one at a time, lifting themselves toward heaven. My parents didn't know me, not really, but they knew I loved books more than just about anything. They didn't know why. Every page of words was a chance for escape, a chance to suicide into a life where the brain was something more than a heavy bundle of gray worms, into a place where the body lost its origins and confines and mutated endlessly. Whole worlds cupped between my hands. The only happiness I ever knew in that space came from between my legs, from a bottle, or from a book. Until the prison filled.

After my brother left, I thought about leaving myself, going to some college with ivy-covered walls, being in closed rooms with men spewing knowledge at me, writing papers that broke open dead worlds and constructed new architectures. I imagined living a double life in college, selling drugs, like him, fucking guys on the side for extra cash. On the edge, like Ophelia, rewriting her ending. After he left, I cried. Then I put my hand between my legs and rubbed so hard I thought I might bleed. Later I used a hairbrush to get at the deepest layers of what was inside me, to get it out, to make it alive and in the room with me, chaotic, heavy, wet, and free.

Nights overtook me. Alone in the attic, my hands dug and carried me into worlds of my own making. I brought my brother's face into the walls now and again, as if he were watching, or guarding, or lifting me into darkness.

The day they lodged the last brick, stretched the last of the chain-link fencing, wound the last barbed loops overhead, I knew that my do-nothing life was about to be over. My dull, dead town had driven away like a herd of lost cows.

It hadn't come easy. My parents had sat numb and silent while others argued their point: There were children in this neighborhood. What kind of lives could they look forward to? What kind of environment would this spread? How could they do this to good, honest folks who worked hard for their money, who saved to build back porches that now looked out on cinder block? But two years of grass-roots petitions, city council protests, and a few stray acts of small-town resistance amounted to next to nothing. In the end those who were against the prison were overcome by those who brayed about five hundred family-range employment opportunities, about business and growth. To the people in the town, it was as if the summer had turned on honesty itself, on everything good and strong, as if something had grown up out of the ground and spread like disease.

What planted the prison in the town was money. The contractor, the mayor, and the governor had a relationship, and despite a few stories on the local news, the town was soon reduced to dirt and hot weather, until the only news stories were about the finishing touches on the penitentiary, and the town was half emptied and wrinkled like the skin on an old man's knuckles.

Our house was at the edge of town, so we were right in the crosshairs. My father had been raised in the oil fields near Port Arthur; he'd nearly gone crazy from the black heads of the bobbing wells, the stench, the slow stab of the drill punctuating everything in sight. When he left, he said, all he wanted to see was land and sky and nothing else—said it made him feel free, the wide expanse. My father, I think, was mourning something more private: The distance of geography. The land releasing toward sky. Who knows what my mother thought? To me she was a frightened doe, her brain wrapped around images of homes for pretty white families, not property for a state penitentiary, not prisoners like a black plague infecting the land.

That great empty expanse my father loved only made me feel dead. In the attic window, with next to nothing on, I'd sit hunched over a shot glass and conjure a kind of dreamscape to fill it. I looked out over the endless rocks and shrubs and imagined red-and-gray structures emerging from the wasteland of dirt, buildings getting born, architecture threatening the sky with its geometry. I watched the fencing contain everything, reaching for miles around the place, its silver crisscrossing and walling off this world from that in great sheets of fence. I'd watch ditches being dug and phone lines being unraveled from huge reels, I'd watch more metal than I thought existed in the universe coming and coming, I'd see them pour the concrete for sidewalks and parking lots. The sound of construction out there in the heat and dry woke me in the morning and covered my dreams at night. I dreamed cities emerging, whole populations breeding from within concrete and steel, an urban species clicking and pounding away like a collective machine. The literal meanings of things dissolved. Dreams took up the space of my reality, dreams rebuilt from the shapes and images crowding up against our little house and family.

The day the prisoners finally arrived was a bit anticlimactic. They came in large green buses, stepping down onto fresh blacktop in their orange suits, marching single file from bus to building, disappearing into concrete and wire and metal. Some of the lines of men had handcuffs, some handcuffs and ankle cuffs, some neither. From my window I built a story: This was a hierarchy of crime—the more dangerous, the more tightly constrained. In reality the men all looked the same, their orange suits smearing them into a single image, their hair and faces repeating endlessly, their footsteps indistinguishable. And the not knowing a single soul, the anonymity of it, nearly made me crazy. Here they were, hundreds of them, soon to occupy tiny rooms and tiny beds in a cage with a toilet and ten steps' walking space, and I had no connection with them, none that was real, none that I could feel. That day I spent drinking and walking ten steps the length of my room, six steps the width of my room, over and over again until I passed out.

When I woke, it was night and my head swam and hurt. I sat up and took my clothes off, went to my window, looked out into the black speckled with stars. A breeze carried my imagination over and through, and I tried to peer in at them one at a time, each sleeping man in a slightly different position, some tucked in curls like infants, others straight as boards on their backs, mouths open. I pictured a man awake like me, trying to see, waiting for something to materialize in front of him, hopeless but resolved. I could see him. I played a child's game: If I could see him, he could see me. I touched myself.

Things went on this way for a while. The penitentiary just out of reach took up all my thinking. I invented a hundred sexual fantasies that involved inmates, torture or escape, violence or the tenderness proffered after a body has given up. I moved from fourteen to fifteen this way, almost dazed; it was as if nothing at all were happening, as if time were thick and dry like the heat and geography. The people I went to school with had no meaning to me. Books continued to house me in a way that the world did not.

The summer of my fifteenth birthday, my brother did not come home. I had a bottle of Jack, a bottle of Gilbey's, and tequila under the bed. I spent my days skipping school and getting high with guys I barely knew, guys I'd met through my brother. The more I let them touch me, the more they didn't mind. From my parents I received a second set of Shakespeare, comedies to go with the tragedies. I count that summer as one that turned me inside out, a snake shedding skin, or just the explosion of a body. By then I had shot heroin a couple times, but that was not my main thing. By then I was making trips from my window to a place two hundred yards away from the fence for long hours at a stretch, waiting in the dark, crouched behind scrub and brush not four feet high off the ground.

They'd emerge twice a day. Once mid-morning, once late afternoon. They'd play ball, walk around, cluster in tight two- and three-person fists there in the yard. I was close enough to make out their figures but not the faces. Faces blurred into little knobs of head, the repetition of orange making me squint. Binoculars helped but also made the dull ache harder to bear. My first distant encounters with the fence of their world came at night, alone, dark, wind, nothing. I sat half hidden by bushes two football fields away. Looking at the patterns of fence, I could feel the hairs on my arms raising, asking, begging. I'd sit out there and drink, and think, acclimating myself to the edge of their world. Then I'd walk home, my feet making crooked tracks, my body not remembering my name, my hands dangling at my sides, fingers itching and twitchy.

All that summer I could hear the electronic drone of the talking heads come through the vents in the house up to the attic like a televised haunting. Debates and news reports and town halls all revolving around the prison, its inhabitants, its dark center. The people on the outside wanted proof that the inmates were doing hard time. They didn't want those convicts, those perverts and degenerates, to have televisions or weight rooms. No luxuries. Doing time is supposed to hurt. Do they expect some kind of special treatment? I remember thinking, Christ, why do people keep asking that? My thinking is, if you can ask the question, you don't deserve to know the answer. Go read *The Tempest*, or don't even talk to me. Someday I'm going to make a bumper sticker that reads: THIS THING OF DARKNESS I ACKNOWLEDGE MINE.

It came to me the day I was skipping an English class, smoking pot with a couple of heads behind the auditorium. Guys who had brothers who knew mine. Guys who by now had put their hands inside me. I was rolling a joint, twirling the paper till it formed itself into something tight and thin and potent, when the idea hit me. It was the most simple and clear thing I'd ever done in my life. I asked where they got their shit; they told me a guy's name, said my brother used to know him; I asked if I could meet him. The whole thing took less than a minute. Convincing the guy about my idea was even simpler. Who would suspect someone's sister, a girl coming to see a man wretched and dismal in his shame? I was already passing as an adult, buying beer and cigarettes at the 7-Eleven, getting into the town bar. My brother had fixed me up with an ID—some girl he met at college. Some girl he probably fucked. I swear to god, we looked like twins, that unknown girl and me, faces echoing each other, two lives touching.

The guy with the drugs gave me the name of the first guy I visited inside. I passed my ID and the contents of my pockets through a slot at the bottom of a Plexiglas window. I was wearing no jewelry, no underwire bra, nothing metal, as I'd been warned. A guard made circles around the edges of my body with a metal-detector wand. My skin shivered. My mouth burned. My lips felt too big. I thought I might cry. But that first time, my body knew a truth that I did not. My legs carried me as if they had memorized the steps without my involvement.

His name was Earl. His gray-blue eyes sucked me up

like I was thin as air. He did not smile, he barely spoke, he put his hand near my collarbone as if he knew me. He was supposed to know me—I was supposed to be his niece, maybe, or his daughter or his sister or maybe just some ripe young thing he'd have killed if she tried to run. His hand moved down toward my waist, squeezed me just under the rib. His face came to me, and his image went out of focus as the blurry stubble on his chin got big and he kissed me, not on the mouth but as close as is possible, wet, hot, lingering there before he withdrew. I could feel his tongue, spittle. He'd deftly taken a small bag from underneath my shirt in back. My spine shivered, my belly convulsed, my mouth filled with saliva. I had to pee so bad it was painful.

I'd never felt more alive in my life.

I saw Earl once a week for about a year.

At night I'd continue my vigils, my hands alive and my body firing its pistons relentlessly. Now I had a precise reason to live; it was as if the world had written itself before me and all I had to do was read it into being. Sometimes during visiting hours in the common room, I'd give Earl a hand job or he would me, and we kept on not knowing each other at all, rarely speaking, and the pleasure was so intense I thought I might die. Sometimes a guard would fondle my tits in an empty corridor. Once an inmate came on my hand while Earl and I were getting each other off.

And all the time I was reading and reading Shakespeare, all the words spinning me into my body, love scenes that turned into death scenes, identities lost or stolen or deformed, good and evil slipping into each other's body, murders and suicides and incests erupting in marriage beds, between brothers and sisters, between the powerful and the enslaved.

In my own bed, dreams wrestled me into color and vision, orange to red to blue and back again: armies of men breaking loose from their rooms, breaking walls and heads and bodies, making inside and outside crazy, blowing the stupid human organization of things to bits. I saw the logic of the inside-out. I knew the world through a body and a mind cut pure and fine as a diamond. I felt as if no other world existed. No other home, no other skin for the body. In books and dreams and inside the penitentiary, between my legs, everything was being reborn.

Night wind changes the structure of things. The distance between my room and the prison closed, as if I had forged a dirt river through craggy desert rocks, my little boat-body bringing me to the other side, not to an idea of womanhood but to a chance to reinvent myself endlessly. I became an expert at the logic of waiting, how it housed the forsaken. Like me, the men in that house had the long wait ahead of them, marked off on the wall in chalked scrapes like tire marks on pavement. Their lives like mine were mutating, their bodies turning from one species to another, from hot-blooded mammals to the cold belly of something with night vision, some animal that could survive in the desert. They knew something from our past about survival and deprivation as a motivation to live.

Whiskey and heroin could keep a girl from letting the dust of a town settle on her, as if they kept the molecules moving around at such a pace that no school, family, daughter-life could close around her. I understood the confines and also the way a mind could be forced to bust them open, its puny rules and knowledges, little gods and the fingers of old women. Sometimes I'd bring pills inside my panties. Sometimes pieces of plastic or wood or dope under the cup of a budding breast. I was at the edge of the world.

I'd like to say I saw it coming, that I'd sharpened my senses enough to expect it. But who among us can see a self? Great minds have failed and failed. And so it was that on my eighteenth birthday I saw my brother in the yard of the penitentiary, his orange suit brighter than the others, his face in full focus, his hands dangling from his arms like a man's so familiar I couldn't recognize them.

At first I saw him as entering a kind of tribe. I wrote the story in my head quickly: He was entering a realm of my own making, a place where reality was not infected with the disease of citizenship or social organization. I felt a kind of pride, as if I had readied the environment in some small way for him. There in the underbelly, I thought we could find a deeper relationship than blood could afford.

The first time he saw me, during a visitation period with Earl in the common room, he ignored me completely. He looked straight through me, his eyes blue-gray stones.

I signed up to see him immediately.

The glass between us, black phones in our hands, eyes locked on each other's face.

"Hello."

Silence.

I was hot and excited. My breath trapped in my lungs. My words flew out in all directions, pinched and condensed through the tinny microphone. "You shocked my shit the day I saw you. What are you in for? Do Mom and Dad know? I don't think they do. No one has said anything. What are you in for?"

Silence.

His eyes crept up my collarbone and rested somewhere between my jaw and my chin.

"It doesn't matter," I babbled on. "How long are you—"

"Shut up. Listen to me. I'm only going to say this once. I want you to hang up. I want you to stand up, turn around, walk out of here, and never fucking come back."

"Don't be ridiculous. You think you're the only reason I'm here? I've been here hundreds of times. It's no big deal. I just thought I'd—"

"SHUT UP. Shut the fuck up." He raised his hand; his fist and its reflection hovered there like threatening question marks. "I know why you're here. I've heard all about it." He paused; his rage seemed to melt for a moment, then snapped back. "What happened to you?"

"What are you talking about?"

"You're famous in here. You're, like, the talk of the fuckin' town."

"I don't know what you're talking about. People here know me. They're used to me, is all. I know the name of—"

"You don't get it, do you? You want to know what they call you around here? Do you? They call you *Hole*. Just Hole." He laughed hard enough for his missing teeth to show. "You're like this child who spreads her legs and humps any guy who wants it. There's pictures of you— little cartoons all over this fucking place. There's little poems about you, about your pussy, the way you put out, how you're a little whore." He picked something out of his ear and looked at it, then back at me. "I heard a guy say you sucked the dick of a dead man."

"You're lying. You're a fucking liar." I stood up. A guard glanced at me. I sat back down. I lowered my voice. "I know the scene here a lot better than you. Look. If somebody said those things, it's a lie. People here know me. Guards. Inmates. They work with me. Give me shit. I sell it. Or I get shit for them. Like you used to do."

"Yeah? Well, how come every guy in here can give a play-by-play description of what you do?" He folded his hands on the table.

Were those my brother's hands? His fingers? I looked at my own hands down on my thighs. They just looked like the hands of a girl. "Fuck you! You don't know me at all. I've got my own life. My own money. I've worked hard for it. I thought you'd be glad to see me. I'm all you've got. I'm leaving soon anyway, don't worry. When I'm gone, no one will know you're here."

"You know what happens to me when they find out you're my sister? I'm fucking marked. I'm a dead man."

I tore loose from his ugly mouth and words like some scared animal. I ran from that room and his hand on that black phone and his voice and his face. I ran down the linoleum hall and past the fondling guards, smirking, laughing, touching themselves, I ran past the check-in desk and out the colossal metal doors I'd seen installed, I ran down the concrete path I'd seen poured, I ran past some men in the yard, orange suits laughing like mouths, I ran against chain-link and sky, I ran to the gate, and it was closed, and I climbed it, I clawed my way up, guards with guns drawn pulling at my heels and tears and spit and my head pounding like crazy. I growled and kicked all the way down, and they were laughing, they saw who I was, and they started laughing, and when they got me to the ground, pinned and wriggling there on the asphalt, saying, "Hold on, now, hold on, we're just trying to help you, damn it, calm down, now," holding my wrists and thighs, I screamed, I took all the voice in me and screamed out to that big sky, to the men holding me down, to all the men in that place I'd given myself to, to the walls, the fences, the whole architecture, I screamed, "He loved me, he did, forty thousand brothers could not with all their quantity of love make up the sum!" and an ambulance came, and men standing in the yard would say later, "That crazy little piece of tail finally lost it," and "Didn't she have a sweet pussy, all pink and sticky like the open mouth of a child, didn't she just?"

A WOMAN
REFUSING

GUY BUSTS INTO THE DINER I'M IN AND BLARES OUT,
There's a woman on top of the Wells Fargo tower somebody get some help! I'm scraping the inside of my coffee
cup with a spoon. The circles grate; people in booths cringe
and look at me. I take my time turning around. She doesn't
need any help, I say. But she's naked! he says, flapping and
squawking. And she's forty stories up—Christ, what if she
jumps? I continue my unbearable stirring. People have
turned their attention to us, a little drama for lunch. I stop
stirring to say, That ain't why she's up there, and then I
start again. I don't even look at him. I can hear his agitation
as he lurches over to me, in my face, and says, How the hell
do you know? He's exasperated. Try being married to her

for a few years, I think. Try living that life for one fucking day. I finally turn and look at him. I know because I've been up there, I tell him. Not just this time. Hundreds of times. And, buddy, I can tell you, I ain't going up there anymore. In Cleveland it was the pump station, in Boston the tower in Harvard Square, in Lubbock the Buddy Holly statue—which is only ten fuckin' feet off the ground. No, sir, this is it. I'm not going after her anymore. I drink the whole cup down in one gesture, like letting all the years settle into one fine, lukewarm caffeinated beverage.

He's not satisfied. Look, mister, he says, I don't care if she is your wife—*Ex*-wife, I correct him—whatever, ex-wife, she's in trouble, and somebody needs to help. We can't just stand by and let—

I snort out a laugh. What I'm trying to tell you is, I was just up there half an hour ago. Talking her down on a god-damn walkie-talkie the entire way up, with a bunch of people I don't know trailing me. You know, strangers are *full* to the brim with advice until an actual fuckin' crisis hits, and then they stand there with their goddamn mouths open like bloated, paralyzed fish.

I get up there, again, for the I-don't-know-how-manyeth time, and she's naked, yet again, and cool as a fucking cucumber. First thing she says to me is, What the hell are you doing here? Couldn't they find somebody more suit-able? Christ. Just for the sake of argument, I say, since we've been through this before, I say, What do you mean by *suitable*? You want a guy in a suit? I laugh. She doesn't. Someone more dramatic, she says, less . . . I don't know, *ordinary*. I look down at the tar on the roof there. Old baseballs, wadded-up paper, wire, weird stuff up there. And I say, Dorothy, I think they assume we have a common history. She looks off and says, Well, *they* should have considered the ramifications of that. I say, Jeez, are things really that bad, that you have to keep pulling stuff like this for the rest of your life? Wasn't it enough for us to go and break up? When I say "that bad," I make the mistake of waving my arms around. She responds by waving her arms wildly and saying, As a matter of fact, *things* have never been *better*. Throws one leg over the edge in some kind of fit. That was the whole marriage—one leg over the edge.

I bet from the ground you saw a helpless naked woman lurching and retracting.

I then make mistake number two. I say, Well, you look great. She says, You motherfucker. She starts cursing so hard that spit flies out of her mouth and her hair rages around like crazy from a wind whipping up briefly. She says, You are the most predictable human being on the planet. You are like Tupperware. Then she makes obscene flailings with the other leg until she's sitting on the edge. My heart is jackknifing in my lungs—old feeling. I move toward her out of instinct, take a moment of comfort in that: Anyone in their right mind would move toward a naked woman on a rooftop if she got too close to the edge. She darts a *You're dead* look at me and says, Listen, don't be such a pathetic ass. You couldn't get me to be a wife. You can't get me down from here. You can't even make me put my clothes back on. You try to grab me, I'll just divorce you in a more permanent way, know what I mean?

All I can do is stand there staring at nothing. I'm so familiar with this feeling that I can barely recognize it: Me like a jerk with my hands dangling from the ends of my know-nothing arms. Me looking at the ground, no matter where I am in my life, no matter what successes, failures, confidence, or panic I may be feeling. We freeze there like that for a long minute, until finally she calms down a bit. A light breeze joins us. You know what's extraordinary? she says. What? I say. You can see flight from above. Yet another completely incomprehensible statement from what always appeared to be a normal, beautiful, intelligent woman. I respond—who knows why, maybe it's inevitable—What are you talking about? I'm tired. I don't want to listen to her nonsense anymore. I am more tired than I have been in my entire life. We're not even together anymore, and won't be. I could remarry, I could have a thousand different lives in a thousand different worlds, and we'd still meet here, like this, in this way. Birds, she says. From up here you see them from the top, not the belly side. See their backs, the tops of their wings. And she holds her hands and arms out like a bird. For an instant I think, My God, she is as beautiful as ever, she is so angry and interesting that she's larger than life, and I think, This is it, this is really it, she's changed, she's different somehow. If the wind blows, she'll lose her balance, and I screech, *DOROTHY, DON'T! FOR CHRIST'S SAKE DON'T*—

She says, Don't be an ass. I'm not a bird.

So I'm going to sit here, and I'm going to drink this coffee, and when I'm done, I'm going to walk out of here, and I'm never going to see her again. I'm still a young man. I've got a life, pal. You wanna save her? Knock yourself out.

SHOOTING

SHE PULLS UP TO A STOP SIGN LIKE BLOOD THROB. *Motherfucker.* She has a flat; she can feel it like a bruised shoulder. Front left. She wheels it over to the curb. Her jaw aches. Her left eye twitches.

Jack. Spare. Tire iron. Truncated lines stack themselves in her skull as she moves. The line *Ten years*. The line *Suffering makes us stronger*. She sets up the metal that will fix her, there on the road's shoulder. It makes a cross. She can't not see it as a cross. The line *Recovering Catholic*. This makes her laugh. She thinks, *Jesus Christ*, then, *Goddamn it*.

First crank. The muscle in her right arm pops up, ready. The cords in her neck tighten. Her left arm dulls over; memory.

. . .

YEAR ONE. Her face down near the pavement. *Skin*, she thinks. Up close the road looks like bumpy, black, magnified skin. She remembers sitting on the pavement, laughing hysterically until the light changed and he grabbed her by the scruff and yanked her back into the car. She still had vomit smear around her mouth, but she was laughing her ass off. Seven hundred dollars, he said. You can't just carry your money around in your pockets like that. Look at it, he said, it nearly fell out into the street there, it's got barf on it, for crissake. She was still laughing. She couldn't help it.

YEAR TWO. I'll pay you two hundred fucking dollars to kiss that guy on the mouth. She waved the cash in one hand like a gray-green fan, steering with the other. Her lover and some guy they picked up on the side of the road. They'd been driving for two hours in some shit-sack place in Texas, and she was bored. Flat flat flat fuck this state, was what she always thought of Texas. Pancake flat. Hand splat on pavement flat. Where do you come up with this shit? he asked, to which she replied, Kiss that guy on the mouth *with tongue.* The two men looked at each other innocently. They were high, childlike. They were more beautiful than was humanly possible. She wanted it. She wanted his mouth on his mouth in her rearview. She wanted man-on-man wet like that. She pulled the car over into dirt and scrub and the lost dry heat of endless sky. She got out of the car. Her boots crunch-printed tracks on that land. She leaned against the red metal, smooth as a drive-in movie. She smoked. She waited for them. She waited for them to meet a woman with a want bigger than Texas.

And they did it. They split her money. Then they all fixed there in the shade of the open trunk, wide open as a mouth. Her eyes went wild like fire. Then closed. Her arm lax. Her mouth open. Her desire a flooded desert. Smile float teeth vertebrae melt.

YEAR THREE. They never spoke of it except to call it "the incident." It started out around nine p.m. They had an epic fight. She slammed the door and left. She went to a bar he knew about but did not frequent much with her. The bar she haunted before she found him: club dancing and sleeping with women. She wanted something back. Or she wanted to be free to shoot around like a marble again. Or she wanted something else.

Inside the bar the smell and the dark and the red vinyl and the sticky black linoleum floor and the regulars and the deejay and her hair, hanging behind her, she could feel it on her back, it comforted her. In a flash she's dancing hard as a boxer with a woman who is thin and muscular and jagged-haired.

Every time they fight, she wants to run or fix.

She remembers the incident. She understands the unsuturable scar it left over his heart. She can see hear smell feel the flash of memory, one scene at a time: His footsteps walking up his own driveway. The windows of the car fogged up. The car seeming to move there in the driveway. What he saw next. He opened the car door. A man was fixing her, but he was also fucking her, his dick was already sliding into her smooth as a needle into its waiting. He grabbed the guy by the hair and yanked him out of the car.

She imagines him showing up at this bar and walking across the floor exactly the same as walking across their front lawn during the incident. She can see him stepping closer to her hair, whipping around as she dances too hard with a woman.

She remembers during the incident how he grabbed her left arm. The needle ripping across her upturned flesh, ripping a second mouth open in the pale and infant-thin skin. She remembers laughing, but there was blood coming from her arm. Her left arm the bruise her left arm the poem her left arm their fucked-up love her arm her past story of herself. Emergency. Emergency room. Her blood cleaned up and put back into her, their love put back into her, her arm sutured and bandaged.

In the club she's dance-humping a woman who'd been her lover once upon a time. She is in full motion, sweat, the pounding of sound, bodies beating each other for all they're worth. She's deaf with desire and wet movement. She's a blur. She's smudging herself into moving particles, a streak of atoms.

And then he is there. His hand there in the club. On her shoulder. Her hair. She spins a bit, then stops, seeing his face in the club mirror. She looks at him, and he looks back for a long minute.

He grabs her arm in sharp interruption. She knows that hand like the back of her hand. She spins round to face him, and his face, and his pulling her outside, and their yelling in a parking lot, and her pounding the metal of the car, and his throwing her against it, and his getting in to drive away from her, and her opening the passenger-side door, and his yanking it closed against her, and her arm breaking there, blue, red, bone, her arm in the door, her arm their life, her bandaged arm shattering like sticks.

YEAR FOUR. Road tripping. Somewhere near the coast. A roadside park. Redwoods and tree needles, and California has a smell. Cooking up mushrooms in a Cup-a-Soup at a picnic table. Cross-country. Crossing country. Landmasses. Flight. Then their bodies began to numb, they yawned, they laughed, colors changed shape, and little vague star shapes clattered at the edges of their vision.

Sitting together, they watched a drunken man climb up the side of the embankment there at the roadside park. He was a Rasta, with a long black ponytail and pockmarked skin; with his rainbow-crocheted hat and sleeveless white T-shirt and khaki shorts, he seemed like a cartoon. He looked a hundred years older than he was. They watched mesmerized as he climbed, pulling on shrubs and branches and shit, getting smaller and smaller as he scrambled up the hill. She laughed, almost under her breath. He put his hand beneath her shirt. Cupped her breast, then felt her nipple between his thumb and forefinger. It felt to him like a ball bearing. Then the man lost his grip and tumbled slow-motion Technicolor back down the hill, head over heels, all the way to the road, where he landed with a splat. Or a bone crash. Everyone, which was just the three of them, kept still for about a minute. Then he stood up and walked away like it was the most normal thing in the universe.

They got their mountain bikes out and decided to ride them onto the freeway. An excellent plan. On the freeway they saw colors shooting by like molecules or corpuscles or DNA strands.

After several hours and some food and some whiskey and an attempt at fucking that turned into a nap, they came back to themselves. They got into the car again and drove off, blasting the Doors on the car CD player. She was laughing. She had whiskey all over her body. She always was clumsy, like a kid. They came around a California-coast turn in the road, and everything stopped. Cars ahead of them with their brake lights on like beady animal eyes all in a row. There was an accident. They saw the ambulance. They saw guys with uniforms carrying a stretcher, broken glass scattered, smashed metal like a disgruntled face. They saw a guy on the stretcher with a big beige neck brace, his skin paler than two-percent milk. He was covered with blood and something the color of iodine, and his mouth, his eyes, had gone slack, as if everything had been driven out of him. His arm dangled off the side of the stretcher; it looked bigger than it should, like a crab claw. She was laughing. Always laughing during the most horrible moments. He wanted to clock her one, but he didn't. Instead he drove them slow as blood beyond this scene.

When they could see the ocean again, he said, What the fuck are you laughing at? How was that funny? She said,

Did you see his ribs? I swear to god, they looked like they'd exploded out of his chest and broken into wings. Did you fucking see that? And he watched her head rock back. And her eyes close. And her needing to say that. And her terrible out-of-whack beauty.

YEAR FIVE.

As you know incarcerations.

As you know the roof of your own mouth.

As you know the fingers you use to touch yourself.

As you know what hurts and what you want to hurt toward pleasure.

As you know the stupid line that does not exist there.

As you know the spit in your mouth.

As you know going down on a woman. Age fifteen. Age twenty. Age thirty.

As you know his mouth will never be her mouth.

As you know his taste will never be hers.

As you know your teeth clenching, wishing, wanting, biting.

As you know the scars you carry.

As you read the Braille of your own body, self-inscription.

As you know the scripts we are given fold in on themselves: This is a woman.

As you know vodka pooling in your mouth better than saliva.

As you know the word "want" as an entire lexicon.

As you know the weight of your left arm, the pull, the mastery of your right hand, the tubing in your teeth, the skill of your fingers at work, the flesh taking the stab, the vein pulsing toward rupture, the breathing slowing in your lungs, the nod, the warm air rushing up your throat, your skull, the sockets of your eyes, you nearly swallowing your own teeth, my god, the knowing, the rain let loose to pure body, her knowing, the first shot received as a child, the not crying, the fascination, the looking up with the eyes of a child at a beautiful man in white, his giving.

This is what a woman wants. This is wanting. Be good.

As you know sentences will fail.

As you know to take a needle and cum.

From that.

Need driving you.

Shooting.

YEAR SIX. Motherfucker. Mother. Fucker. The phrase "detox for Recovering Catholics." They gave her a room-mate with red hair. She wanted her. She watched her in her sleep and masturbated under white sheets. Her hands alive and unflinching. The redheaded woman became her need. Her drive. She lunged, propelled herself across their room, over linoleum and white, over sterile and clean—too clean—shock-backed floors and walls.

Turned out the redhead was awake too. Sweating. Corpselike in a pool of herself. Breathing in rapid bursts. Her hands on fire.

They devoured each other, nearly, like animals locked up.

Next day they would sit in a semicircle with other women, black circles under every eye. Most were smoking. Legs thrown out in front of them at odd angles. Mouths, eyes, all saying resist resist resist. Hearts saying fuck you fuck you fuck you fast or slow.

She would think goddamn it, then lines that mimic that phrase: Dogs have it, Go bang it, Fuck bag it, Gun big it. She'd laugh. Is something funny, L? Did you have something to say? Do you think maybe laughter is your cover story? Huh? Let's hear about it. C'mon. Show us some guts. Take a risk for once in your life. Tell us something we don't know. You mad? You got some rage in you that you think is special?

Cunt throb it.

Hand ram it.

Lead blood it.

Goddamn it.

She was forced to stay an extra four months for carving

GODDAMN IT into her arm with a sharpened and resharp-
ened pencil.

THE LOST YEAR. She was in the parking lot of Our Lady
of Little Flowers Church. She was there for a commitment
ceremony. He asked, What's a commitment ceremony?
She called him a dumb fuck. It's when two queer people want to love each other in public. He didn't say anything, then did. She'd been clean nine months. Does it
mess with you? What? That she's marrying someone else?
Someone not you? Or that you married me? Is that it? Was
that it? Does that make you feel incarcerated or something?

All she heard in her head was blood pounding goddamn
it goddamn it goddamn it, driving her crazy, making her
brain propel itself down the rivers of her body into the
veins in her arm into lines like what is a woman what is a
woman what am I?

YEAR EIGHT. Driving in the desert. For all she was
worth. With her whole body. Her mind gone wild. Her hair
like fire. Her cells dividing, in rage or love or just plain
need. She drove most of the year. Or at least it seemed
that way.

. . .

YEAR NINE. What was shooting? To cause to be projected, to cause to fire, to kill by doing this, to wound by doing this, to put to death with a bullet as punishment, to hunt, to destroy or move with a projectile. To project something forward, out, toward. To direct with the rapidity of a moving bullet. To put into action. To detonate. To photograph. To increase in speed. To flash across the sky. To dart painfully in or through a part or parts of the body.

YEAR TEN. Pulled over on the shoulder. Flat tire. Her ordinary arms change a tire on an ordinary car. Then into her vision comes somebody pulling over. Was it her hair that drew them, driving out in blond tracks against the sky? It is a man, she thinks, a beautiful man, his hair long and windblown. He gets out of his car and from the knee down his legs get bigger and bigger. When he is a foot away from her, he stops. Then and only then she looks up. Up from the black leather boot to the bottom cuff of his jeans up his shin to his knee to his thigh up his denim to his cock. Then up his belly his torso his collarbone she pictures under his T-shirt and then up to his jaw his mouth his eyes. His whole face. Then his lips. They could be anyone's lips. They could be hers.

"It looks like you could use," is all she hears.

She lets this random man help her even though she doesn't need. His arms working are beautiful. His hands. The insides of his arms. His veins cording across his arms more familiar than his face.

When he is finished, he says, "Do you want to score?"

And it hits her. Shoots through her. The past wants. Like a mouth salivating. Like a cunt begging. Like the weight of an arm. Like the next sentence. Like a faith that won't be arrested. The past can break her body no matter what, can move her, propel her, speed her, drive her open, the past's needing, no stopping it.

She bends down to tend to the tire. She screws the new tire in tight, pockets the wrench, slips back into her car, and drives.

A WOMAN
APOLOGIZING

SHE SHUT THE SILVER CUFF ROUND HER RIGHT wrist. It was done: wrists cuffed to brass. All there was left to do now was wait; 5:25, or 5:45 at the latest, if he missed the first train. Her wrists clanked against the brass bedposts. She pulled her arms out away from the bed, and her wrists just clinked, trapped, secure, something she couldn't quite name. She smiled. She rattled her little wrists. She put her chin to her chest and looked down the length of her body. Her breasts flattened like fried eggs, each slipping toward its own armpit. Her rib cage rose and fell. Her belly dipped down like a flesh bowl. The curls of her pubes crinkled up toward air. She could feel herself becoming wet already. She spread her legs as far apart as they would go; her lips sucked open, the air opened her, she wiggled her toes in delight. She grinned at herself, by herself, to herself.

It had been, after all, a terrible argument. His face was darker than she had ever seen it, his teeth clicking between his words. He had been shirtless. Yeah, she had thought, he's pumping up with anger at me, pulsing toward rupture at me, to me, about me. And she was angry as well—her too-pale skin all blotchy at the neck and chest, blood booming in each ear. She saw her own hands flare and fan in front of her like deranged birds now and again. She screamed so hard she felt the cords in her neck strain and screech, almost cracking against themselves. What a fight, one of those wonderful horrible ones.

She knew he was right. She *was* a control freak. It was true, if she asked him where he wanted to eat and he told her, inevitably she would say, Well, we *could* go there, but the wine selection is so much better at this other place, and he would of course agree. If she asked him what he wanted to do and he said, How about a movie? of course she would say, All right, but then we'll miss the free jazz in the park. If he wanted eggs, she asked for pancakes; if he drove the car, she knew a better route; if he wanted to be on the bottom, she clamped his hips between her bony little knees and tugged until he rolled to the top; and if he wanted to be on top, she squirmed out from under like a

chipmunk escaping a cat. And when he said, You don't
understand what it's like to be black, she would say, You
don't know what it's like to be a woman, and there was
nothing he or anyone else could say to that.

But that day he'd just *had it*, he said, and he threw a
glass of gin to the floor when she said, *Jesus*, but she was
tired of having to decide everything for the two of them.
The second the words left her mouth, she knew she ought
to suck them back in, but it was too late, and he just
snapped. And then she really blew it: She said, as if she
didn't know not to, You must really feel a need to attack
me. And then thought, What a jerk. Why can't I just let the
fight go on naturally? Honestly, just quit the debate tactics
and listen, that's what he always told her, and he was right.
She didn't want to lose him, after all, he was the only good
thing in her whole rotten life. If she could just develop a
self to police the self that kept screwing up, a little invisible self that could stop the real her just in time.

So after he grabbed his blue shirt like a flag and slammed
the door shut on her, she was left sitting there with her
marvelous anger and her stupid control. She bit the inside
of her cheek as hard as she could and closed her eyes tight
enough for tears and pounded the top of her head, saying,
Dumb, dumb, dumb.

She tried to think how to apologize—make him stir-
fry and flan for dessert? spill rose petals from the door to

the bubble-filled bath?—but nothing felt serious enough. How to make it up to him, how to exorcise her controlling witch-self?

How proud she was when she finally thought of it: an act of total submission. What sweeter gift could a controlling woman give a wounded man? She was so excited that she ran out that minute, caught the subway up several more blocks—they'd been there dozens of times, admiring the nipple clamps, fingering the leather, faces flushing at the plugs. They loved these stores, loved to be in them, loved to buy gels and magazines and arcane contraptions and then go home and work each other into lather and sweat and dripping delirium. She remembered the night they bought a piercing kit—how she squeezed the skin around his nipple, how the beautiful dark bump rose like a kiss toward her, how she slid the silver point through to the other side as their foreheads pressed together. She remembered the night he bent over her like a tender archaeologist, how she sat up on her elbows trying to see, though all she could really make out was his furrowed brow, his eyelashes, the top of his head, his fingers working as the point went through her without a sound. And then, when he was finished, he dipped his sweet dark face down into the sweet dark mouth, mouth to mouth, she would never forget. She bought the cuffs and ran all the way home, dreaming of their new forgiveness.

Five-twenty now, and she was hot all over. Soon I'll be sweating, she thought. Her wrists twisted loosely inside their cuffs. She felt the tingle between her belly and her spine. Almost by accident she noticed the buzzing voices and shifting images of the TV. She had forgotten it, so busy she was staging herself, trying to decide where to put the keys (between her legs), what position her legs should be in, throwing them around to find an alluring pose. But now she realized she'd left it on the twenty-four-hour news channel. It's fine, she thought. Something mindless to distract from the waiting.

She had to hold her head a little to the side, peer around the bedposts, but she could make out what was going on. What was going on was war. *Which* war was difficult to say—the sound was barely audible, so she only had images to go by—but it was a wintry place, close-up shots of soldiers showing icicled mustaches and beards. The men looked pale blue and dirty and tired, more tired than she could imagine. Some of the faces were talking to the camera, and though she couldn't hear any words, she could see their beaten faces, resigned to something beyond sight. A village peppered with bodies, bloody snow. A dog sniffing at potatoes spilled from a bag clutched by a bulky bundled woman, her head shrouded in a flower-printed scarf. All perfectly dead, fallen where shot, knee-deep in snow in the middle of their lives.

Whatever war it was, it soon gave way to panels of heads and mouths and waves of commentary. The mediascape of winners and losers and statistics, of men and women in suits, as if their pin-straight hair had wiped this week's war off the screen.

She closed her eyes and bit the inside of her cheek, because it was 5:40 and he wasn't home yet and she suddenly realized she was freezing.

She looked up at the ceiling, down to her nipples standing up against the cold, over to the window now black with night, but the TV kept pulling like a hungry child. Five-fifty and she had to concentrate, had to distract her imagination to keep it from slipping into the nasty mind-wander of paranoia when your lover is not in the doorway. Now a tingling in her flesh: Was her own skin trying to tell her something? She jerked her wrists in a kind of death rattle against the slow fear crawling up her spine. He's stopping to buy a bottle of wine, a rosé. He's getting cash to take her to dinner. He missed the first train, he ran into a heavy crowd, the sky opened up and thickened the air, everyone outside is walking in slow motion.

By six she was really cold, and the shivering was taking all her energy so that her brain wouldn't work right. It kept stuttering and lurching, and out of frustration she went back to the TV. But the TV hadn't changed at all, it was the same news, or different news with the same faces, as if all over the world the news had the same actors: gaunt, icy faces, bulky women falling into death, sniffing dogs, eyes that were always black, buildings blasted beyond architecture. Why hadn't the news changed since she last looked? Who were these actors in wars that never ended? She grew agitated over the repeating images, until she finally decided she would stare at the set until they changed. There must be sports news, after all. Or bad weather. Weather always changed the picture.

But they just kept coming and coming, six-fifteen, six-thirty, and when she finally closed her eyes and shook her head, trying to shut them out, she realized she was shivering. At seven she wept, slowly at first, but by seven-thirty she had snot running down her trough and all around her mouth. She was saying his name in low, whimpery wails, she was losing the feeling in her arms, her fingertips were prickling, she was quivering and hiccupping and shutting her eyes from the TV, the awful twenty-four hours of news, the news and the cold and the cuffs and the loss of circulation and the waiting that could be the rest of her out-of-control life. And he kept on not coming home, and if he didn't, then what?

MECHANICS

HOW'D YOU GET THE NAME EDDIE?

She's eyeing my name tag. From the get-go I feel her contradiction. She says her husband usually brings the car in, and sure as shit she's got a stupid diamond on her ring finger, but she's also all lash extensions, lip stud, push-up bra, and full sleeve of tats on her right arm—classic femme. Maybe the husband is a cover story.

Father gave it to me, I say, continuing my work. Edwina.

She moves closer. Most people drop their cars off, throw their hands up, walk away with that please please please don't let this cost an arm and a leg. I don't know what she wants, but I already like the way she wants to stick around and watch, to see what's going on, even if she doesn't get it. I mean, when she came into the garage, she told me, The car makes a strange sound when I shift the gears. What kind of sound? I asked. This is usually where people make asses of themselves, trying to sound like a sick motor. But she said, You know that noise you hear when your alarm goes off in the morning, only you're not awake yet so you don't exactly hear it, you sense it, something between a buzz and a ring, and for a moment you don't know if it's a hangover or a dream or the phone or the alarm or an insect or a snore? I had to admit I knew what she meant. I overslept a lot. Didn't help me worth a shit to guess what was wrong with the car, but it did make me curious. She knew what she was talking about, even though she didn't.

So when she came over to where I was under the hood, I said, Could you hand me that lug wrench? She picked the tool up and looked at it a long time before she handed it to me. She got some oil on her hand, and she looked at that too.

I worked on her car. She stayed very near. So, she says, how long did it take you to learn to be a mechanic? Now she is making circles with her ring finger in a blob of oil near the battery. She's leaning right under the hood with me.

Better watch all that hair, I said, then answered: I picked it up real fast. Think I had a knack for it. I've been around a garage all my life, it seemed natural. My dad owned a garage. The oil, the smell of gasoline, the chrome, the black innards of an engine. I was helping with repair work by the time I was twelve.

Were there other girls helping with the repair work? she wants to know.

I laugh. Nope. Just me.

Now she's fingering the tools. She's asking me their names, what they're used for. It's the sort of conversation that makes you feel good about what you know.

I kind of start enjoying the company. I mean, I still think she's a little weird, like when she starts asking me about the engine parts. She says, Don't you think they're a lot like body parts, like that tube over there that curls underneath that other thing looks like intestines, and that thick curved thing like an arm with a flexed muscle, that big thing in the middle with all the compartments could be the lungs, it even looks like it's meant for air, and all of it together here under the hood, and us inside it tightening and screwing and greasing.

So now we're both oily and curious, I guess.

When you were a kid, did your dad teach you other things? You know, like how to throw a baseball?

Not really. Just mechanics. He was real busy. What about you? You look athletic. Those are some shoulders. But I'm lying. My father taught me how to be the man of a house.

I was a very good swimmer.

Good for you.

I guess I was a tomboy. I didn't have many girl friends. Except for two. One was a cheerleader. The other was a girl nobody else talked to. She had red hair and glasses. She used to sit by herself under a tree all through recess.

I just keep working, even though by now I'm getting horny. I guess it's the weirdness, the unexpectedness of her. Everybody gets excited by things they aren't expecting. Not that she scared me, not really, except that now I see she's holding the lug wrench and swinging it a bit. I've read stories, you know? Women are doing strange things these days. I think, Don't be silly, don't be so paranoid. She's weird, not crazy.

Then she says the weirdest thing of all, just out of the blue. What do you think about pain? she says.

I play it cool. Don't like it, I say. And it's true. In my life I'm all dom all the time. I have no interest in any other role with women.

Not even a little? Like when you get a back rub and they hit a really sore muscle and it hurts where they rub it but you just can't get enough—what about that?

Now, that shit is funny. Delayed-onset muscle soreness—DOMS—is the pain and stiffness that your muscles feel for hours after exercise or even a massage if your body isn't used to it. The soreness is strongest for up to seventy-two hours after the exercise.

Well, I guess everybody likes that. Th' fuck? Is she messing with me or what?

And what about fear?

Now the tools are kind of slippery in my hands, and I start sizing her up, thinking if I see her raise her arm at me even a centimeter, I can swing this monkey wrench around into her stomach, just hard enough to scare her; after all, I'm bigger than she is, could pin her to the garage floor easily. But the second I imagine her really trying to hit me, I realize that I'm wet and throbbing and she's just setting the tools back down like the most normal person in the entire universe.

What do I owe you?

She stares at me.

My thighs ache, and it makes me feel like someone besides myself.

SECOND COMING

WHY DID SHE DO IT? I WOULD SAY THAT SHE DID IT out of love, for me. But not your ordinary kind of love. She is a very selfish person. Probably the most selfish I know. For example, I'm not sure how conscious she was of the despair I'd experienced in those years. I don't think she understood what I was going through at all. But she always had a kind of primal intuition about pain. Even when she was a kid, if someone was suffering in some way, she'd run in and try to save them. Injured people, cats, dogs, moths caught inside trying to get out, someone crying or just lonely; once she even designed a sling for an old oak tree with a broken branch. And if you were to look her in the eye and ask her for something, I mean even if a stranger did, I don't think there is anything she wouldn't do. Homeless people on the street had big nights because of her. Once she helped a crazy guy get loose out of a side gate at St. Mary's. So when I asked her, there was a logic to it.

The day I asked her, I had no idea in hell where to get the equipment I needed. I had a book with directions on proper procedure and a list of things I'd need: plastic cooking basters, syringes, tubing, rubber, oil. She had several different sizes of syringe. I don't know why I didn't think more about that. I only felt lucky not to have to go and purchase one. She had one that was the perfect size. We did end up having to buy this plastic-cap gizmo with a hole in it that fit over my cervix. To contain the little devils and increase the chance of success.

Another item that turned out to be incredibly useful was her vibrator. When she asked me if I wanted to use one to get off first, I just looked at her blankly. Don't you know what a vibrator is? she said. I didn't. That figures, she chuckled, younger sister has to teach older sister how to use a sex toy. We laughed. When she brought it out, I blushed. What are you supposed to do with that thing, I asked, stick it up there or what? and then we laughed some more, and she told me that when the time came, she'd show me.

If a woman is going it alone, there are several strategies she can use to increase her chances of success. I didn't have the money to set up a procedure at the clinic, so I was giving it my best shot. One thing that helps is to stimulate the organs, as during intercourse. The increased mucus and swelling help to prime the vagina and cervix. You know, like motor oil. Another thing that helps is to get into a position where your feet are higher than your ass. Like yoga. Makes sense, doesn't it? Mixing the semen in warm water in a cup helps the semen collect so that it sucks up into the syringe well and disperses evenly into the vagina. Once the semen is inside, it also helps if you remain in that inclined position so the little fellas don't leak back out. Details.

My sister's husband was in the bedroom, watching TV. I was propped up in my reverse incline on the living room couch. She'd bought this great deep red blanket for the occasion, and I nestled down into it. She'd arranged candles, incense, and flowers everywhere; the room was heavenly. She convinced me to take all my clothes off. I just need to be naked from the waist down, right? I said, but she said, You may as well get some pleasure out of this, and that seemed right. She put on some Celtic harp music, which made the room a little dizzy, unless it was the red wine she convinced me to drink. My skin was warm. Sweat was forming underneath my breasts and between my legs. She brought the vibrator to my hands and turned it on. I didn't really know what to do with it, so she guided my hands. At first she touched my lips with it, and I had a deep and to-the-bone tingling sensation throughout my body. She pushed it down to my clitoris for a few seconds, and my entire body spasmed; then she withdrew it quickly and touched it to my breasts, my nipples, one at a time. She then moved it down again, and at a certain point she let go so that I was guiding the movement. My eyes were closed, my hands were alive. I was breathing very hard. At a certain point, I opened my eyes; they felt puffy—my lips too—and I looked at her. I was rocking my hips and moving my hands, and my scent rose up between us, and I was looking at her. She was smiling and staring between my legs, and I liked her staring there; then she looked into my eyes, and I felt the deepest need for her to say something, and she said, Touch your tits with it again, and I did that, and then she said, Now put it back in your pussy, move it around . . . and then I closed my eyes again. I think I heard her whisper that she would be in the bedroom and that I should keep going.

While she was there, I heard moaning, and I came shortly after that. When she returned she had the cup full and I was wet and flushed and filled with my own desire turned in on itself.

She nestled herself between my legs in a kind of kneeling position. She filled the syringe without my noticing. She told me to close my eyes. She tickled an imaginary line down my body from my breasts to my pussy with her finger. Then two of her fingers entered me, and she rubbed around in circles. She said, Can you hold your lips apart, wide apart? I did. I throbbed so hard between my legs I thought it must have looked like a mouth opening and closing. I closed my eyes again. I felt her fingers there still, and then I felt the syringe enter me, but she had her fingers around it in such a way so that it was unbearably gentle. I bit the inside of my cheek. I felt the overwhelming urge to beg her to do it harder, then I felt crazy, then I shot that thought out of my brain. I did not feel her expel the syringe, but she was moving her hand and the syringe in and out when she did it.

When I opened my eyes, I had tears. I saw her head and face between my legs, the light of her blond hair, the heat of her skin, her mouth, open.

Later we all had dessert and watched a movie.

I remember the day she was born.

BEATINGS

HIS FACE HAS THE LOOK OF A BOXER'S MUG, BUT only in certain light, particularly in winter, when shadows and darks and lights stand out in stark contrast to one another. Only when winter gives way to a single barren tree against an almost white sky, or a boulder shoulders its own outline against snow. His fighter's face emerges or recedes according to the light. So do his eyes, the cups of fatigue underneath each yielding to the flattened spot just above the nose, the jaw clenching and unclenching itself while he's eating or fighting or fucking or sleeping. You wonder where you've seen this face before, and then you think it looks like the faces in those movies, men beating back the world, De Niro in *Raging Bull*, Stallone in *Rocky*, Brando in

On the Waterfront. The more you watch him move, at night, working out, pushing the body against darkness and winter cold, the more it's true, it is the film of a man and not the man, or it is the man caught on film repeating himself. Any image of a man that is against itself, that you suddenly see is any image of a man. In some ways men are always fighting the image of themselves in the world.

Outside in the gray, he works out. Boxing. Short pulses. He faces off against what is called a body opponent bag. It is in the shape of a man's torso. The man's face has the look of an aggressor. He hits. The blows land in the head, the chest.

In his mind ideas seize, recede, then again raise and rise. Fisted speed dug deep and jab extended until it is shot strung back to the shoulder. His thoughts a never-ending drive and end, and end, and end, and end.

INSIDE THE HOUSE, where it's light, he wraps those same hands around a bow and strings and plays. His hands change shape holding the cello, like birds moving from the dull land to the winged sky. A metronome marks time with ticks, with rocking, with regular, adjustable intervals. Its measures and rules give meaning, sense, divisions, and designs to sound. The metronome unvaryingly regular, undergirding the music, with its variable rhythms, melodies, harmonies, and counterrhythms. His hands cup the instrument. His fingers carry the crouch of a dream in which chaos orders and slows and sings. The strings as thick as the bones of a hand. The reverberation bellows up through his wrists, forearms, shoulders, into his spine.

In winter, even the trees are beaten. Gray of asphalt to gray of fence post to gray of field of dormant growings. Gray of the tips of branches and trunks, gray of the hills' hues dulling over, gray of the edges of things against the gray-white sky. Like color is bruised, bludgeoned, dead.

Up close, his fingers on the strings look like something out of a dream. Suddenly the knuckles are fluid and seemingly without joints. The fingertips ride hard and wide; they tremble, then go taut. The white skin stretching between fingers seems more like an infant's than a man's. And when the strings pulse and reverb, it is as if the instrument is of the body, not a wooden, hollowed-out object. Between his legs its singing rises. From his spine the tones pull up and out. Against his chest the neck presses; even his teeth resonate. The wood grain as deeply brown as his eyes. The notes rebody a body. You must close your eyes.

Cadence—any cadence—is what saves him. A rhythmic flow, as in poetry, as in the measured beat of movement, in dance, in the inflections of a voice—all modulations and progressions, moving through a point beyond sight, sound, vision, being. To fall, in winter, without ending.

.   .   .

THE MIDDLE OF THE NIGHT. He is thirty years old. He gets up to pee, then crashes to the floor in the bathroom. His wife finds him. He is having a seizure. He is not conscious, though his eyes are open. She lifts his feet slightly even in her fear, holds his head in her lap and says his name and says his name and says his name until his eyes flutter open, like a fighter coming to. That's how his life became this fight. That's how his fighting became him. When he works out now, you see the fighter taking form. His fight is with his father. His fight is with himself. His fighting so familiar he cannot recognize it, like a face in the mirror after shocking news.

His wife—what is her part? She thinks of all the men in her life. Her father, heart disease. Her first husband, heart murmur. Her second husband, liver and heart disease. Her first husband's father, heart failure. Her second husband's father, heart attack. Her father's father, heart attack. Everyone has seen this movie. Any movie today must take what has been told a thousand times and give it a form no one expects.

She is a decade older than he is. She had thought of herself as the one closer to the far edge of life, closer to genetic undoing. But it is now that she sees the death in all of us. What she has begun to see is that we are all an audience watching the image of someone fighting. What she has begun to learn is the black and white of slow motion. If she stands at the window and watches him working out, what she sees is a frame at a time. One move following another. The fist pulled back to the shoulder, then—a separate movement—launched at the false body of the opponent bag.

Zocor decreases triglyceride levels. Aspirin thins the blood. Fish-oil capsules and flaxseed oil wage enzyme war against the body's fatty walls. Arteries and blood roads and blued vessels bulge and thin in heavy rhythms. A glass of wine each night, once pleasure, is now prescription. Red meat torn from animal, the old instinctual longing, is replaced with white rice, broiled fish, food for bodies hairless and light. He obeys the regimen. He fears the weakness that may attack his bulk. He cannot picture himself; he is afraid he is changing in ways he cannot live with.

HE DECIDES THAT he will begin to film himself working out and playing cello. At first he doesn't know why. Later he decides, or realizes, that the films will be for his son.

He never had any home movies of his own childhood. He never knew his father. Everyone these days takes color home videos on their phones, but he shoots on old-fashioned black-and-white film. The rushes hang in strips down the bathroom door, then coil onto white reels. He tells himself that he and his son will watch them together, as movie stars do in private. The images living and turning forever like old movies of prizefighters. He remembers something someone once told him: that the last scenes of a film determine whether you want to watch it again.

She watches him work out. She admires the violence with which he fights, because he is finding a place to put the violence, a form that is beautiful.

We believe in fighting, somehow, still. We want to see the raging bull, the boxer beaten by a tragic flaw. We cheer for Rocky; we want to see a man's love bring his violence to life, see his fighting save him and provide a happy ending, the sequel, the sequel. We want to see a fighter who is forced into labor that is not his own die a heroic death. We want to see him maintain his integrity even if it kills him.

Aikido, karate, judo, tae kwon do, arts of combat, of beauty, of sport, of self-defense, of speed and thought, of the body unbodied from its tasks and let loose into movement and rhythm, arms unarming themselves, wrists cocked back to fluid animal rotations, shoulders dipping and curling, neck forgiven its upright burden and relearning the side-to-side and back-and-under tricks of instinct, chest and biceps pumping and bulging like meated masses, hands letting go of tools and becoming not a part of the body but the body itself, of all the internal organs in symphony and not against one another, not individuated but of continual measured movement, as if the entire corpus was what drove things, and not the heart alone.

HE DOESN'T KNOW IT, but his numbers are improving, the good cholesterol beating the bad, the fats fading in sebaceous white waves. He doesn't see it, but his weight is dropping, muscle, spine, and nerve replacing the old soft buffer between the world and his heart. For isn't it his father's body he has inherited? He doesn't feel it, but his heart's beating is no longer against him, though he fights as if everything, even the moon, were against him. Still, inside his body, invisible, his heart is finding a rhythm that will bring him life, calm, like the soft pink of an open palm.

What is it? What was it? Why? His father dead at thirty-three. Heart attack. The blood blocked, the oxygen cut off. The muscle, that fist-shaped meat, unable to breathe. His father. Thirty-three. Heart attack. Words like thrusts. And all that living up and through him. What is it? What was it? Why? His fists asking.

He is working out in front of the house. His fist connects whap-smack solid with the heavy bag. He catches a glimpse in his peripheral vision of his wife and son inside the house, as if they were a heart inside a body, smelling like infant's skin and milk. Then he strikes a blow straight to the chest of the false body. It is a kind of hope, this beating.

A WOMAN
GOING OUT

LEAVE THE LEGS FOR LAST.

Take the razor up smooth against the slight resistance of stubble, flick the wrist at the top, dip the head into the water, swish it around, then back down to the ankle for the next run. Flesh smooth-appearing in a track through white foam. Do it again. Expose the leg in stripes of skin.

Wash off the excess foam, squeeze aloe and rub briskly between the palms, *ahh*, warm caress up and down the legs.

Slide the hand in each leg, spread fingers wide, and examine for runs, point one toe and enter the hose, pull slowly up the ankle, the calf, and over the knee to the thigh, pause; same with the other leg, pause; scrunch it inch by inch up the thighs to the balls pushed back up into the cave, to the penis tucked tight between the legs and se-cured with a thong and over the hip bones and snap the elastic around the waist with thumbs.

Then the pumps and the jewels: red stilettos and rhine-stones in the ears, at the neck, and of course on the wrists.

HOW TO
LOSE AN I

DO NOT RUB FROM THE NOSE TOWARD THE SIDE OF your face. Always wipe toward the nose in a horizontal direction.

HIS EYES ARE CLOSED. Wait, no. His eye. Just the one now. He picks up the phone. He dials. His skin is too hot against the headpiece. A woman's voice says, "Hello," then he speaks, then she says, "Jackson?" This voice resting him. His heart beating out *thank god thank god thank god*. She says, "Where are you?" He responds, "Can I see you tonight?" Then he nearly passes out.

He does not know how to explain why he needs to be in the car. He thinks up a hundred absurd errands a day so that he can drive around until dark. Maybe he needs that movement to hold him in place. When he sits inside at home, even the air looks empty. The whole world looks slightly off. As the change is not within him at all, but instead the world has changed its angle of vision, closed in on itself, defocused. Isn't that the damnedest thing? Perhaps the line of a road is the only thing that will ever make sense to him again.

It makes him horny to drive to Mary's house. They have never been lovers. They will never be lovers. He doesn't fuck women. Not that he hasn't, just that he doesn't. Mary makes him horny because their way of knowing each other has lasted twenty years. She is a big woman, Amazonian, manlike except that this makes her unusually feminine, in a European way. Because she gives him back rubs that last two days. Because she can't cook and he cooks for her and it makes her cry to eat. Because they are both neck-deep in their lives and have no idea how to proceed. Because they both ended up in California after swearing not to. Because she will not leave him, ever, did not, in the hospital, slept in a chair, like a woman waiting in a movie. Because she has little scars all over her body from a car accident years ago, little glowing white feathers covering her torso. Because their suffering is stronger than love. Because she will look him in the eye. Because she is the only human he has seen in months who will do that.

THE ORB ITSELF has no surrounding connective tissue. A CONFORMER made of silicone is placed inside the socket following surgery to maintain orbit volume and to help form cul-de-sacs or lid pockets that will hold the eye in place.

HIS DRIVING DOWN her dead end, his hearing the car door shut *whack*, his feet carrying him down a path he could walk with his eyes closed, his knocking on her door, her letting him in, their kissing, their looking at each other, smiling, then her eyes traveling down his body, then her saying, "My God, look at that!" Their laughing their heads off.

Their eating the pesto and pasta he cooks. Their getting high after dinner and his taking his patch off. Her fingers soft as whispers, his flesh hollow. Their watching videos until three a.m.—*Red*, *White*, *Blue*—and then their falling asleep, tangled bodies on the couch. Her saving his life, him saving hers, and no one else seeing it.

THE COLORED SPOT goes up, under the upper lid upon insertion.

. . .

HE DOESN'T WANT to lose his way. That's why he bought the maps. Six of them, just in case technology fails him. Funny—each one is slightly different from the others. How can that be? You'd think there'd be some kind of consistency, some standard. But he finds a street on one and not another. He finds a bridge on one and not another. He finds sites listed on one and not another.

He'd bought the maps as part of The Plan. The Plan was to drive cross-country, to get back his mojo, his self-worth, to get in the car and reclaim his goddamn self. Mary had heard from her therapist that "healing journeys" were important, and she was going on and on about a possible trip to Europe, and he spit out, "What about a road trip? What if I took myself on a road trip?" And Mary had said, "That's pretty loaded, Jackson. You sure about being in a car for something like that? Stuck in a car for that long?" And he'd said, "I love cars. I love road trips. I've always felt more myself when I'm driving—when I'm inside that movement." She paused a moment, then said, "Maybe that's just right. Maybe revising the story in a ritual like that, like driving, would be just the thing." Then she'd looked him in the eye and said, "Go."

The Plan was for him to drive from Seattle to California

to Arizona to New Mexico to Texas, through the rest of those southern states, all the way to Key West. To drive it without stopping and capture it on film, a frame at a time, to replace the nightmare with something real. In a car not the car that had killed Michael, not the car that had taken his eye, but a new car he would get now. Beyond any of that.

AFTER YOU WASH and rinse your hands, lift the upper lid with the thumb or forefinger of one hand. Next, slide under the upper lid and, while holding the prosthetic in place, pull down on the lower lid.

WAKING UP IN THE NIGHT, cold sweat, like a big fleshy cliché of a self. Did his whole life leak out of the socket that night, or only part of it? His memory bends in on itself like a video stuck on pause. Even when he shuts his eyes as tight as possible, the images continue, perhaps stronger than ever, sometimes so fast he can't watch, can't breathe.

In the morning he makes a list of things to pack, even as his mind races ahead:

Boxers ten, jeans four, T-shirts ten, socks ten; sweaters and fleece three, leather jacket one, sunglasses brooks brothers, button-downs gap, running shorts nike, caps two; aftershave, deodorant, electric razor, beard and nose attachments, toothbrush, toothpaste, travel-size baby shampoo, l'occitane conditioner, lotion and bath milk, first aid kit, q-tips; water, scotch single malt five bottles, money, camera, film, eyes.

In the afternoon he packs the car. Mary comes over to help, and afterward, as she waves good-bye from her car, he thinks, She looks like a bird, some great prehistoric bird dipping its wing before taking flight.

In the evening, when it's cool and the road whispers its blue-black beg, he drives.

Do not be *alarmed by tears and secretions. Simply wipe toward the nose with a tissue or warm washcloth. You can also use Johnson's baby shampoo and Q-tips for cleaning dried secretions from the margins. If thick secretions or excessive tearing occur, call the emergency hotline.*

Yes, within motion is the only place he feels normal. Driving is best, next to that, swimming. There is something about the way a car holds you, about shutting the doors and the seat cupping you like a hand and the steering wheel presenting itself to you as if you could control things like direction and speed. Speed comforts him too, as if it were all of existence reduced to one element, a fundamental feature of existence.

With water it is floating. The way water carries a body. Weightless.

At first the road trip is like a photo essay. He keeps having simple feelings: Now I am crossing the border between Washington and Oregon. Now I am on the Coast Road. Now I am changing speed zones, highway to suburban area to city and out and up and faster again. He keeps having feelings like: I'm passing the same landscape for the second, third, fourth, fifth time. At first he sees only small changes. Then geographic ones, the hills a bit more browned from the sun, the trees less evergreen and more eucalyptus or palm. Smells seem more telling. He is driving, and California has a smell, orange trees and asphalt. He is driving, and the hills give way to ocean, sea air, and exhaust. He is driving, and memory moves his sight, his hearing, his heart beating.

As he leaves the West Coast, the windshield is a giant body—no, it's just the California hills giving way into the Southwest desert, like great shoulders or the well of the small of a back.

But the body filling the windshield before him is always the same. No matter what he stops to take pictures of, all he hears is the clicking of the camera—no phones for him, he loves his solid old camera, the way film looks—its eye blink-ing machinelike, its shutter putting boundaries on light and speed. No matter the shot—red earth of New Mexico, red-woods of California, road signs and vistas, moonlight on ocean—all he sees is Michael thrown from the car, his shirt ripped open, biceps and chest cut clean through, Michael perfect, Michael perfectly still, Michael shot from the car onto the road, eyes open for the rest of his life.

During the drive, he realizes that the film he's using has pictures already burned onto it. You know how it hap-pens: camera gets left sitting around dormant, film gets developed, time is suddenly out of whack, and suddenly Christmas comes up against summer, the new entertain-ment center against the black-tie event. Driving past image after image, he is seized with the memory—a fact, clear and cutting—that somewhere on this roll are pictures of Michael.

His mind numbs itself. He considers blinding the cam-era with his fist. He considers throwing it out the window. He ends up putting it between his legs, its lens pointed up to him, its glass eyeing him questioningly.

He wakes up in a hotel crying, his tears salty and damp. His eye still cries—what is he supposed to think of that? He just lies there in the dark thinking, I am not blind. He isn't exactly thankful, just observing. He looks at the ob-jects in the room, like shadows of themselves in the dark:

A chair. His bags. The television. He grabs the remote and clicks, holds the remote to his dead eye without thinking. He rubs it over the hole without thinking. He touches it to his mouth without thinking. He falls asleep with the little electronic gizmo clenched close to his cheek.

He wakes in a hotel in Tucumcari, bolt upright, tight like a car jack, teeth clenched. His eyes are closed, but he can still see the flashing red lights of the ambulance, or the fire truck, or the cop car, or all of them, or just retinal splashes gone berserk, or blood in his eye, or how the hell should he know?

He wakes up in a hotel in Pensacola. He's left the window open all night so that he could hear the sea. He is smiling a little. He gets up to pee, pees, looks in the bathroom mirror. Mild nausea. He looks down at his eye in a hotel glass filled with saline solution. It looks back. His chest tightens; he does a breathing exercise until it loosens again. He leaves the bathroom, turns off the light, leaves the eye submerged and displaced.

TOO MUCH HANDLING *can cause socket irritation.*

A FRIEND HAD TOLD THEM about an oyster bar called One-Legged Pete's. They should go there, he said, for the view, for the scene, and for these big buckets of crab legs that suck so sweet your lips ache. All those double entendres that used to be playful and sexy lodge in his jaw like nails now. He gathers up the pictures he has taken so far, his camera, and his wallet. Then he goes back into the bathroom and rips off two inches of white surgical tape. He places it where his eye should be.

IT IS NOT NECESSARY *for you to wear a bandage.*

AT THE BAR he thinks how right the friend was. He thinks how much Michael would have liked it, Michael the more outgoing one, the more playful one, the one with the *GQ* smile, Michael the already tanned don't need to go to fucking Florida one, Michael the well-hung, the fucking god in bed, the one who never cried. Blue eyes. Two. Perfect as water. He looks out at the ocean, pictures them swimming in it.

At the bar he takes his pictures out. He looks at them closely, one at a time. Whatwhatwhat has he been taking pictures of? Things anyone could see from a moving vehicle: Road signs, big farm fields, lines of trees. Shots of hills garroted by telephone wires. Images of strip malls and gas stations and truck stops. One in particular baffles him: license plates, for Christ's sake. VI9 GBD, New Jersey. PLC 306, Colorado. IAFB228, California. HOT ROD, Nevada. Is HOT ROD why he took the picture? Was he drunk? He doesn't remember. He does remember a conversation they had, about how lucky they were—that neither of them was sick, or likely to be; that both had been careful and precise sexual partners before they got together; that both were young and ready to commit and make a life together stretching out like the fingers of a human hand. He is seized in the gullet. He cannot order a bucket of crab legs. He wants to wade into the sea up to his eyes and cry.

MAKE CERTAIN TO USE *all the medications prescribed to you.*

THOUGH HE HAS CONSIDERED turning back every single day since he left, just as he has considered suiciding every single day since the accident, he keeps going, and a day comes when he reaches Key West. The heat of Florida has dulled his senses. The taste of scotch is permanent inside his mouth; he can taste it anytime he presses his tongue against his inner cheek. He checks into a beautiful white hotel named the Conch House. The linens smell heavily of fabric softener in a way that comforts him. The walls are white. The furniture is white. Everything is clean like brushed teeth or sheets.

He sits out on the pool deck in a white wicker chair. A hotel attendant brings him a piña colada. He spikes it further with scotch. It tastes like shit, but he doesn't care; he is relaxed and drowsy, his eyelids are heavy with almost-sleep. He is wearing his eye. His camera is in his lap. He has in mind a short nap and then, as the sun sets, a walk down the main drag for photos. Breathing in the thick wet heavy of Key West, he comes close to dozing.

An enormous splash snaps his lids up, to reveal a beautiful blurry sea creature; no, a statue fallen into the pool; no, a young man tanned and slippery surfacing from a dive. His hair is black and sheened as a record album. His skin the color of Albuquerque sand. His eyes unbearably onyx and open. If there is something that Jackson does not want a photo of, an image of, it is this young man. If ever something could be violently true of his life, it is that a photo of this young man might kill him. Even taking the picture would be like being shot in the face. He is overcome with this feeling. It is horrible, this beauty. He begins to cry, and soon he is weeping uncontrollably. Worse, the young man sees him and begins to move toward him. As he comes closer and closer, till he's as large as a cinematic close-up, his lips torturously full, even the bridge of his nose excruciatingly perfect, he begins to surrender. His skin goes slack, and his jaw gaws some, and his heart stops jackknifing, and it is then that his camera slips to the concrete with a little cracking *tink*.

"Oh, man, you dropped your camera," the young man says. "I hope it's not damaged. Lemme wipe my hands off. . . . There. Let's have a look at it."

He turns it over and over in his large hands like a sunken treasure.

"Oh, Jesus. I think the lens is cracked. That's terrible. Those can be expensive to replace. Stay here—I'll go ask up front if they know of a repair shop. I'm sure they can find you one."

The lens is glass. Old-school.

And with that the young man and his camera are both gone.

IF TOO MUCH TIME passes before fitting, the socket may begin to shrink and it may become more difficult to achieve a satisfactory cosmetic and functional result. If too little time elapses, not enough healing has occurred to achieve a proper fit.

BACK IN HIS HOTEL ROOM, he locks the door. He shuts the drapes. He turns off the light. He doesn't ever want to see the boy again. He doesn't want his camera to exist. He hopes it spontaneously combusts. He'd rather die than open the door to the knocking brown hand of the beautiful young man holding the idiotic and horrible camera out to him, saying, There, I had it fixed, it works like new, now you can take all the photos you want while you're here, and would you like to have a drink to celebrate, the hotel has a bar, maybe dinner if you're free, if not that's fine, just thought some company might be nice tonight, and where did you say you were from? He catches himself looking at the back wall of his hotel room for a way out, but all he sees is the mirror.

What was he thinking? He wasn't ready for a trip like this. He wasn't ready for human interaction. He is suddenly surprised he's made it this far without another crash. He pours himself a drink, sucks it down, then reaches up and pry-sucks his eye out of its socket. It tumbles to the carpet. He picks it up and puts it in his mouth. He considers swallowing it.

What it comes down to is this: He feels trapped inside this white room with a dead eye and a self he cannot bear and a set of memories more alive than his present. He feels as if the kind man will come back to kill him at any moment. He feels as if there is no escape. He thinks, I will die here one way or another. He picks up the phone and calls Mary, gets her machine—Mary, Mary, I'm lost, I'm drunk, I'm tired—I don't know how to do this. He realizes how in crisis he sounds. He sends her a hundred texts saying some version of I'm fine. It's fine. You know how dramatic I can get in hotel rooms. Everything okay. All good.

Hours pass. He has no idea how many. Things grow darker. He feels his own edges dissolving a molecule at a time.

Eventually there is a knock at the door. He looks at the door, one-eyed and weak, then walks over and opens it.

The flash is whiter than the mind can imagine. "Surprise."

The shutter releases him; things go back to gray. It is the young man, smiling the way men do before age captures their faces. "It was no trouble at all. Turns out there's a shop right around the corner, and they had a glass lens, used but not a scratch on it. I got you a good deal. But now I'm afraid you owe me dinner."

Jackson stands there, more innocent than the present. Something happens, then, in the frame of the door there. As if his memory had been released from his brain, pouring out of the hole in his head. He follows the words, slow and dumb, taking orders. This beautiful man has taken his picture in Key West, Florida. In the doorway of the Conch House, a hotel. The beautiful man has repaired his camera. The beautiful young man wants dinner. He gives up entirely.

After dinner they walk along the night beach with their pants rolled up at the ankles. Eventually they undress and slide into the black water, warm as the body's fluids, salty as tears. They float on their backs. He looks up at the roof of the world and thinks, This is exactly what it looks like when you close your eyes. Only the stars are different.

Store in water *or saline solution.*

THE NEXT DAY he wants to be in his car, but differently. It is dawn. He dresses and leaves the room. He takes his camera, goes to his car, and drives down to the beach. No one is there. He keeps driving. He drives onto the sand, even though cars are not allowed. He keeps driving. He drives up to the lip of the sea. Then in. Slowly and without alarm. Only a little ways, until the wheels are submerged. He opens the car door and steps out. He leaves the car there like that, the camera in the driver's seat. Let the sea take it.

He sees the body of his lover, floating like kelp, beautiful, rhythmic, not mangled from the shot through the windshield, not splayed with arms and legs bent wrong.

In a day or two, he thinks, the young man will leave. Jackson will sell his car and live on insurance money there in

Key West for as long as he can. Perhaps he'll grow a beard, even wear a patch. It will be all right to go this way, to live in a kind of sleep or shortsightedness, in a place where the road ends in the sea, as if its motion could be cupped forever—since any other life would drive him to his end.

TWO GIRLS

THEY ARE SIXTEEN AND SWINGING, SWINGING HANDS
and the hands hold the wrists of sixteen and swinging,
around and around and dancing their feet in the sand in
circles, in circles at edges of sea foam and dancing and
swinging at sixteen, and swinging are girls of sixteen with
hands holding wrists and wrists held in hands they are
swinging, they are circles of round and around and the love
of sixteen and swinging is sea foam, and the foam is their
mouths into smiles and mouths making laughter at light
and swinging, making laughter at light and the bright of
her teeth is the bright of her eye is their heads rocking
back into love and to sea foam, and the sea is their hands

and the sand is their hands and the hand over wrist to the wrist over hand is their swinging, they are sixteen and swing and the song of their love is the sand and the sea foam, and no one is looking at two girls and circles and out of the world into spiral and flight.

ACKNOWLEDGMENTS

This book simply would not exist without the heroic efforts of Rayhané Sanders and Calvert Morgan.

All love and enduring gratitude to Brigid, Andy, and Miles for keeping me afloat.

Thanks to art and heart comrade Lance Olsen for the endless creative lifeline spanning years.

And to everyone anywhere who lives in the in-between of things: I get it.